TOBIAS JONES

The Salati Case

D1353318

ff

faber and faber

First published in 2009
by Faber and Faber Ltd
Bloomsbury House
74–77 Great Russell Street
London WC1B 3DA
This paperback edition first published in 2010

Typeset by RefineCatch Limited, Bungay, Suffolk
Printed in England by CPI Bookmarque, Croydon

A CIP record for this book
is available from the British Library

ISBN 978-0-571-24586-4

2 4 6 8 10 9 7 5 3 1

For John Carnegie

Monday

I was looking for Via Repubblica 43, but the fog was thick. I could barely see the doors, let alone the numbers. I had got a call out of the blue an hour ago, asking me to go and see some notary called Crespi.

Eventually I found 43 chiselled into the stone at head height. Below was a brass rectangle with black letters: ARMANDO CRESPI, NOTARY.

I rang the buzzer and a female voice gave me directions over the intercom, 'left-hand staircase, fourth floor'.

The wooden door into the palazzo was so large that there was another smaller one inside which now clicked open.

I walked up the stone staircase slowly, not knowing who Crespi was or what he wanted.

'Permesso,' I said as I walked into an opulent front office of walnut wood and burgundy leather.

The receptionist looked at me. 'Castagnetti?'

I nodded. People only give me my full surname when things are formal. Everyone else calls me Casta.

'Please have a seat,' she said. 'I'll let Dottor Crespi know you're here.'

I sat down and looked around. There was a business newspaper placed at the centre of a round table. On the

3

walls were dark oil-paintings. The whole office felt formal and old fashioned.

The quick click of the woman's heels on the marble floor announced her return. 'He'll be with you shortly.'

A few minutes later a short, white-haired man came into the reception area. 'Castagnetti? My name's Crespi. I'm so sorry to have kept you waiting. Please come this way.'

The notary led me down a wide corridor and held a door open for me. He motioned for me to sit down. He went behind his desk and leaned to his right to open a drawer and pull out a folder. Every movement seemed slow and precise. He put the folder on the desk between us and laid his thin fingers on top of it.

'You're a private investigator, am I right?'

I shrugged. 'I offer my clients clarification.' That was what I always said. 'Offro chiarimenti.' I clear things up.

He looked at me through narrowed eyes. 'You look younger than I expected,' he said.

I shrugged again. 'How can I help?'

He smiled briefly. It looked like a muscle spasm. 'A client of mine passed away on Friday. She has left a testament which is—'

'Name?'

The notary paused to acknowledge the interruption. 'Salati, Silvia.' The inversion of the first and second names was deliberately formal. 'For reasons of the correct disposal of her estate', he went on, 'it is necessary to certify as to the legal status of her younger son, a certain Salati, Riccardo. He was reported missing in the summer 1995 and is almost certainly deceased. But his

4

legal status is currently "missing". My late client's estate can only be distributed if that assignation can be changed to "presumed dead".'

'You want me to prove he's dead?'

'The will requires that,' he held up a letter and pulled on his glasses. His voice went up a semitone to indicate that he was quoting from the old lady. '. . . due investigation should take place to reconstruct exactly what happened to my younger son Riccardo.'

'Younger son? How many children are there?'

'Two. The older brother being Salati, Umberto.' Crespi raised his eyebrows at me like I should recognise the name. The legalistic inversion of surname and Christian name was beginning to irritate me. 'He owns Salati Fashions on Via Cavour,' Crespi explained.

Another clothing boutique. By now, almost the only shops left in the centre of town are those selling speed-stitched cloth from the Far East.

'This isn't a murder case, Castagnetti. All my client would be commissioning you to do is to verify the legal status of the subject.'

'You need a "missing" turned into "dead"?' My tone was at odds with the mellifluous phrases of the notary, who paused again, as if to acknowledge my vulgarity.

'All you would be required to do', he stared at me, 'is to form an opinion upon whether the man in question is dead or alive.' He threw his palms upwards, as if to say that it was the simplest task in the world. 'If I may say, Signora Salati was a client of mine all her adult life. I personally saw the devastation her son's disappearance had upon her. This isn't merely a request to help with

5

archiving a case; this is a chance to allow a kind, honest woman to rest in peace.'

It was quite a speech. The notary looked pleased with it. He was nodding his head slowly with his eyes reverently shut.

I thought it over quickly. It sounded like an unpromising proposition. I preferred the fresh cases, where there was hope. The old ones meant faltering memories and no happy ending, if there was an ending at all.

'Big estate?'

'That is confidential and, if I may say, irrelevant. Suffice to say that it's the standard estate of a woman who had been economically comfortable for thirty years. Allora?'

'And the terms of the will?'

'The terms of the will have no relevance to your investigation. In fact, it's precisely the opposite.'

'Meaning?'

'She left an open will. Which means that her executors were given the facility to rewrite it according to the results of your investigation. Her will requires independent proof of her second son's status before her estate is disposed of. That disposition is determined by whether or not the boy is "missing" or "presumed dead".'

I hate notaries. Each one creates their own refinement of arrogance. Not even Crespi, I thought, would be without an interest.

'Tell me more about the case,' I said.

The notary drew breath. 'I know very little about it. The subject in question disappeared from the train station on the night of San Giovanni 1995.'

'When's San Giovanni? August sometime?'

The notary looked at me, surprised I didn't know. '24 June.'

'No police investigation?'

'His common-law wife in Rimini reported him missing three days later. The carabinieri filed the report and that was that.'

'They didn't investigate?'

'There was no evidence of a crime having been committed. And Riccardo had a bit of a history of disappearing. They were reluctant to waste public money looking for a man who had a habit of being, shall we say, on the road.'

'No sightings since?'

'Nothing.'

I looked at the meticulous little notary who was uncapping a fat fountain pen as if to draw up the contract.

'My standard fee', I said, 'is two thousand euros per week. I take five thousand up front to cover expenses. I report and invoice on a weekly basis.'

The notary jotted the figures down hastily and stood up to shake hands. 'My secretary will issue you a cheque for your expenses.' He passed me a card so I passed him one back. 'Come and see me in a week's time. Chiaro?'

'Chiarissimo.'

Back on the street I tried to think in straight lines. Silvia Salati had died only a few days ago. They had to find Riccardo not because there had been some sighting or contact, but simply for routine. Riccardo's mother had died and there was an estate to be distributed, nothing more. The case was as cold as the Salati woman. It seemed actuarial, not human: it was about the direction of money, not about the whereabouts of a man who had probably been dead a good decade.

The more I thought about the case, the less I liked it. I knew that my report was expected to be just a rubber stamp, something that was needed in order to release funds. I wasn't expected to solve something, just to tick a few boxes. There were bound to be 'interests' in the case. There were always 'interests' that slanted things, external pressures which tried to push it in one way or another.

The old woman had presumably left something: a house, maybe a few savings. Her heirs would be more interested in finding Riccardo dead than alive. Someone, and it was probably Umberto Salati, would be hoping I could prove as much. That way there was one less person with whom to share the estate. Not that that made much sense if the widow died poor.

I headed towards the centre of town. The damp claustrophobia of Padanian fog sucked the colours off the city. It felt isolating because you couldn't see more than a few metres ahead. The place felt so humid that even the cobbles seemed to sweat.

I tried to walk on tiptoe to move my stubborn, busted ankle. It always got worse in winter. The weather seemed to stiffen it up and I spent my time drawing circles with the toes of my foot, trying to loosen up the rigid scar tissue. It had happened a long time ago.

Someone had tried to give me a foot massage with a security door. I didn't walk for a while.

I looked at the blurred people coming towards me through the fog. Women in egg-shaped fur coats. Men with pencil goatees. Orange buses and elderly cyclists.

It was a strange city. It had been transformed since I was a boy. There used to be old eccentrics living in town, the descendants of families who had lived in a particular *borgo* since Maria Luigia was Duchess. Children played football in the cobbled backstreets. There had been artisans: the carpenters and cobblers and tailors. Now, though, everyone had moved to the suburbs. In the centre there were only clothing boutiques and phone-dealerships selling glinting handsets made you-know-where. The rest were banks and legal offices and various 'authorities'.

But somehow the city had retained its charm. It was cut in half by a river and that meant you could only reach the other side by using one of half a dozen narrow bridges. They became arteries where you saw friends and friends of friends. It was a city small enough for coincidences to happen and where everyone had some sort of connection to everyone else.

That was why I liked this time of year. It was the only season when the place offered anonymity. Visibility was reduced to twenty or thirty metres, and for once you could limp around without fear of being recognised. This was the only time you could really go about your business unseen.

Not that I really understand what my business is. I

have no company, no headed notepaper, no staff. I don't advertise. Now I think about it, I don't even know how Crespi got hold of me.

But I'm always busy. There's always employment for someone who lives off the dirt. And I do the dirtiest: fraud, missing persons, anti-mafia, *omicidio*. The only thing I don't do is infidelity. I don't mean in my private life, because there's no one there to be unfaithful to. I mean I don't snoop with a telephoto, trying to prove that people are putting it about. I don't do it because it's sordid and sad and – like the fog – it's all the same.

But that's how I got started in this line. That's how everyone starts off. Marina, an old friend of mine from way back, thought her husband was cheating on her. She said she was certain of it, said she wouldn't even trust him to put out the rubbish any more. He denied it until he was red in the face, swore on his blessed mother's life that he would never betray her. He used to get furious with her, said she was demented.

She was telling me about it one day and I just offered to find out. As soon as I said it she was gripping my hand, pleading with me to give her back a bit of certainty in her life. She said she would arrange to go away one weekend and we would see what happened. Half an hour after her man had dropped her at the station he was unbuckling another woman's bra.

Before I knew what was happening, every cuckold in Emilia-Romagna wanted my help. That's how I discovered I had a talent for something useful. I could give people the truth. I found I had a talent for getting to the heart of things, for finding out about what had been hidden or covered up. I had a half-decent radar for deceit. People began to bring their injustices to me, perhaps because they sensed it was a subject I understood. They brought me their terrors and their tragedies. 'Where is my wife?' they would plead, or 'Who killed my daughter?' I never understood why they asked me. Maybe they asked everyone and I was the only one who offered to help.

And I don't know why I did. At the beginning it might have been kindness, looking into troubles because some people seemed to have an unfair amount of them. I listened to their stories and asked questions in return. Question after question until someone didn't want to reply.

But it's not kindness any more. I've seen what polite people can do and I don't trust politeness or kindness any more. It's just a job and I do it for the money. And I take the money because the costs are so high: after a few months in this line you lose trust in everything. When you've seen that much betrayal and deception, you can't trust what you see, let alone what you don't. Everyone becomes a suspect. Mauro says that's why I'm no good with women. I always look for a motive, and when someone says they're in love, that they're living without an ulterior motive, I worry about what they're really up to.

I waited for a pause in the traffic to cross the road. Cars loomed out of the damp cottonwool air and sped past. I felt my ankle throbbing and leaned on my right instead.

I decided to go and look at Salati Fashions and turned

into Via Cavour. It was there on the right on the way to the Battistero.

Through the shop window I could see a man who looked like the proprietor. Salati must have been mid-fifties. He had a thick grey moustache which covered the top of his mouth. It was yellowing on the right-hand side so I assumed he was a smoker. He looked thick set, like he had rounded out in recent years.

I watched a couple walk into the shop and Salati was on them, offering help, pulling hangers off the rails. I watched the way the man smiled at the young couple. He put his head on one side, a move that made him look as manipulative as a six-year-old in plaits.

The couple left the shop and I heard Salati offer them a curt *buongiorno* as if he were saying get lost. I walked through the door before it had sprung shut.

'Umberto Salati?'

'Yes.'

'I'm Castagnetti. I'm a private investigator.'

Salati hesitated and tried to get his eyebrows to touch. 'You're the person who's going to verify,' he paused out of delicacy, 'as to the status of my brother, is that right?'

'It is.'

'He's already hired you?'

'Crespi? This morning.'

'Tell me your name again.'

'Castagnetti.'

He looked aggrieved.

'What did he tell you?'

'Nothing.'

'How did he find you?'

12

'I didn't ask.'

He clicked his tongue and walked around the shop shuffling hangers. He looked nervous. 'You know someone is trying to pretend Riccardo is alive?'

'How do you mean?'

'The mourning notices in the paper today. . .there was one from Riccardo.' He must have seen me perk up, because he quickly tried to damp down any excitement. 'Riccardo's not alive,' he said, holding my stare. 'Someone wants us to think he is, but he's long gone, I'm afraid.'

'So why would someone pay to publish a mourning notice in the newspaper?' I asked.

He shrugged. 'That's your job.'

'When did she die?' I asked quietly.

'Friday.' He looked up at me as if trying to work out why I had asked.

'I'm sorry,' I said quietly.

Salati sighed. 'At least we saw it coming.'

In my line, I thought, it's always coming. Only difference is, I'm supposed to do something about it. I looked up at Salati and he looked tired. I knew what it was like to lose a parent because I lost both a long time ago. Salati was in a bleak place.

I looked around the shop. There were light pink jumpers and shirts with extraordinarily large collars.

'Coffee?' he asked.

'Thanks.'

'Laura,' he cooed to his young assistant, a girl whose body was perfect but for her cantilevered nose, 'could you make us a coffee?'

There was something gentle in the way he spoke to her and I wondered if they were lovers. Most of the shopkeepers ended up taking their pretty assistants out for dinner as a prelude to showing them the finest hotel rooms in Romagna.

'You're not closing for lutto?' I asked.

He shook his head. 'It actually helps having something to do. We're closing up later.'

Laura was out back now and I decided to iron out what I knew. 'The night your brother disappeared, he was waiting for a train back to Rimini, right?'

'He had bought a ticket. Some people came forward to say they had seen him buying a ticket.'

'And then?'

'Nothing. He was supposed to be going back to Anna in—'

'Who's Anna?'

'His woman. They had a daughter, my niece.'

'Called?'

'Elisabetta.'

I was writing down the names. 'Anna what? Salati?'

'No, di Pietro.'

I wrote it down. 'Do they still live in Rimini?'

'Last I heard.'

'You're not in touch?'

'On and off. Not as much as back then, but sure, we talk occasionally. Anna and my mother weren't close.'

'Why?'

'You would have to ask Anna. But they didn't get any closer once Ricky went missing. The opposite. Once it

14

was clear Ricky wasn't coming back, we saw a lot less of her and of little Elisabetta. She was two I think when it happened.'

'And what brought Ricky back this way that weekend?'

'He had just come to see my mother in Sissa for the day.'

'Sissa? That where you're from?'

'Right. She had driven him back to the station, dropped him there. I think that was another reason it hurt her so much. She blamed herself for not staying with him on the platform until the train came. As if you had to wait with a twenty-year-old. He would have thought it ridiculous, and so, in other circumstances, would she. But because she never saw him again, she felt it was her fault that she had just dropped him there.'

'What time, do you remember?'

'She said it was twenty minutes before the ten thirty train.'

'And she drove off as he went to buy a ticket?'

'Sure.' He said it like he was still defending her.

'Where will I find Anna?' I changed tack.

'I told you, Rimini.' Salati's tone had altered now. He clearly felt he alone was left to defend his family's honour.

'Any address?'

'I'll go find it.' Salati stomped out to a back room and I looked at Laura, the young assistant. She had come back with two plastic thimbles of coffee. She looked at me and held the tray out.

'Thanks.'

Salati returned with a piece of paper: 'Via dei Caduti, 34. Rimini.' He took the other coffee and smiled at the girl.

'What were you doing', I caught Salati's eye, 'the night Ricky disappeared? 24 June, wasn't it?'

Umberto looked at me and laughed nervously. He was about to say something, but then wiped down his moustache with his thumb and his forefinger and looked at me again. 'You don't waste time do you?'

'Who were you with?'

'Roberta.'

'Your wife?'

He nodded. 'My ex.'

'Anyone else with you two that Saturday night?'

'Just the two of us. I think she was due that weekend, or the one after. I can't remember. We were just sitting there at home waiting.'

'Your first?'

'Yeah. Daniele.'

'How many you got?'

'Two boys.'

'They still in the city?'

'No. She took them back to Traversetolo when we split.'

'Why was that?'

'Why did she go to Traversetolo? That's where her parents were from.'

'No, why did you split?'

'Roberta and I?'

I threw my chin into an upward nod.

'She didn't give a reason. Just said our marriage was over.'

He didn't look particularly wistful about the separation. If there was any pain there, I guessed Laura eased it nicely. He seemed like so many of the middle-aged men I met in this city: a financial success and a family failure. One out of two wasn't bad, I always thought. I would settle for one out of two.

I looked around the shop one last time. I turned over one or two labels. The prices were written by hand with an ink pen. Salati saw me and took a shirt out of my hands and rubbed the cloth between his thumb and forefinger and started explaining the quality of his stock. His fingers looked, like him, slightly chubby. He obviously liked the finer things in life. He was a bon viveur, but then everyone was around here.

'I'm going to make some enquiries', I said, 'and come back to you. Buongiorno.'

I walked out quickly. I didn't like getting sucked into idle conversation with suspects. As soon as they offered you something, they would be asking for something in return. I heard Salati shouting goodbye to my back as if I were one of his customers, but by then I was back in the fog, enveloped in its icy white cold.

I crossed the road and walked towards Borgo delle Colonne. It was one of the few colonnaded streets in the old city. Protected from the rain, and close to the inner ring road, this was where the city's prostitutes used to wait for their clients at night. It had been a bohemian haven when I had moved in here ten years ago, but the whole area was now being made 'signorile' and the prostitutes had been moved on to the motorway slip-roads. I missed their ugly honesty.

I walked up to my flat and sat at my desk. I rested the phone between my jaw and ear as I dialled the familiar number of the carabinieri.

'Dall'Aglio? It's Castagnetti.'

'Good morning.' He paused. 'What do you want?'

'I'm reopening a case. The disappearance in 1995 of a young man called Riccardo Salati.'

'Silvia's son?'

'Exactly. You knew her?'

'Vaguely. I heard she died last week, is that right?'

'Yeah. It's about the will. This boy disappeared in 1995. It would have been the Questura that dealt with it.

'I remember. And what do you want?'

'The name of the officer who took the report, his present posting, and any documentation which you might have in the records regarding the case.'

'That all?' He laughed. 'It's very busy here, I doubt anyone will have time to look into it until this evening. I'll get someone on it when I can, and I'll call you back by the end of the day.'

It went on like that for an hour. I phoned everyone I thought necessary. I phoned the town hall to ask if I could distribute the photocopies of the missing boy. I had to fax my request, so I typed up a letter. I made a note to ask Umberto Salati or Crespi for a photograph. I phoned every school in the city until I found out which ones Riccardo had attended. I phoned the secretaries to arrange visits.

On a whim I decided to phone the only doctor listed for Sissa. A secretary answered the phone and eventually put me through to the doctor. I introduced myself and the man started buttoning up.

'An investigator you say?'

'Sure. I'm after just a couple of—'

'I can't tell you any details of any of my patients. You understand, confidentiality . . .'

'Even the ones who are dead?'

The man didn't say anything and I pushed it.

'Silvia Salati.'

'Silvia? What do you want to know about her? She only died last week.'

'How?'

'How did she die?' The man breathed out loudly. 'Nothing confidential about that. It was her lungs. She had been a smoker all her life.'

'Nothing unexpected?'

'I told her thirty years ago it was going to happen.'

I thanked him and put my finger on the phone cradle and lifted it again. I listened to the dialling tone, thinking about what to do next. I opened my diary and found the number for the library.

Long beeps followed long silences.

'Emeroteca,' said a young woman's voice.

'Have you got La *Gazzetta* from the last few days?'

'Sure.'

'Open shelf?'

'Sure.'

'You're open all morning?'

'Until five tonight.'

I dropped the phone in the cradle, stood up and pulled on my jacket. I walked the back way, along Viale

Mentana and Viale Piacenza, coming at the library through the Parco Ducale. It was a small building, but quick and efficient. A girl, the one I had spoken to by the sound of her Roman accent, fetched the two *Gazzettas* published over the weekend and passed them to me in a pile the size of a child's mattress.

I took them to a desk and laid them out in front of me. I took the Saturday edition and opened up the paper.

It was winter and the sports section was full of *calcio-mercato*: the transfer gossip surrounding the big teams. All the important clubs and names were in bold so that you could read all the likely deals in a few seconds.

I turned over another page and saw a wall of faces staring back at me. These were photographs of the people who had died in the last few days. *La Gazzetta* must have been making a mint out of mourners. I knew how much each inch cost from when I had lost a friend a while back. The *necrologi* were money for old rope.

Most of the photographs looked as if they were taken when the deceased were in middle age and they made the paper like a throwback to the 1970s. There was something about the faces, the thickness of the glasses and the length of the hair, which looked out of date. Alongside each photograph or name were expressions of mourning from relatives and friends.

There was no mention of Salati. She had probably died too late on the Friday for anyone to publish a mourning notice on the Saturday. I took the Sunday paper and flicked through it to the pages of the dead. Almost a third of a page was dedicated to her. There were thirty or forty rectangular inches of sympathy from relatives and friends, each announcing their deep regret. Everywhere the name Silvia was written in bold like one of those footballers about to be transferred.

There was a photograph of her, a black and white shot. She looked purposeful: a thin necklace around a tight jumper. A good-looking woman with a determined mouth.

I read through the names of those who had publicised their sense of loss. They were just meaningless names to me but I would get copies. My work was all about methodology. I would cut out every mourning notice and arrange them in some kind of alphabetical order. Many of the mourners wrote only first names, so it wouldn't be an authoritative index of her kith and kin, but it was the closest I could come up with for now.

I walked to a side room where they kept the day's papers and found the *Gazzetta*. I went to the *necrologi* again. There were more mourning notices expressing regret at Silvia's death, fewer this time, but there were still a dozen or so.

I scanned through them and immediately saw the name Riccardo. I read the sentence above it. 'I am devastated by our loss. I will always carry you in my heart. Your son, Riccardo.'

I looked at the words again. 'Your son, Riccardo', it said.

My immediate reaction was the same as Umberto's. Nobody comes back from the dead, I thought. That was make-believe. This read more like someone who wanted to cloud an inheritance.

But it clouded my case as well. And if this was a

phantom Riccardo, I would then be chasing two ghosts instead of one.

I asked the girl to photocopy the Sunday and Monday necrologi. She looked at me and sighed quietly. 'One euro and twenty please.'

I passed her some coins that she dropped in a wooden drawer. She put the papers under the machine and a lime-green light moved across the paper.

'The papers from the 1990s, are they back there as well?'

'*La Gazzetta*?' she said over her shoulder.

'*La Gazzetta*, summer of 1995.'

'It's on film. Which months do you want?'

'June, July, August.'

She gave me the photocopies and then opened the front desk and went back into the stacks. She came back with three large rolls of film and walked me over to the old-fashioned machines for viewing. She put one roll into position and fixed the other end into a slot and ran it forwards. She flicked a switch and the film was projected on to a large screen.

'Backwards, forwards,' she said, showing me the buttons for scanning through the month's editions.

I thanked her and she walked back to her desk. I was both expectant and subdued. There might be something here that could give me some background, but it would probably just be a waste of time. Most of my work involved wasting time.

I started on 24 June. I went through the paper scanning the headlines. The first few pages were normally national and international news. I turned to the inside pages that ran small stories about what was going on in the city.

On 29 June I saw a small paragraph in a side-bar of information about shop opening hours and parking discounts. There was no photo and no byline. It was an appeal for information: SISSA MAN MISSING, ran the headline:

> **Riccardo Salati went missing on Saturday 24 June.**
> **He was last seen waiting for the Rimini train on**
> **platform two of the railway station. Anyone with**
> **information is asked to contact Colonello Franchini**
> **at the Questura.**

I wrote down the name Franchini and quickly moved to the subsequent papers.

I went through the next two months but there was nothing. I would have to talk to someone on the paper, one of the reporters, see if they remembered anything.

I gave the rolls of film back to the girl and walked out. Just as I was reaching the road my phone started tickling my leg.

'Castagnetti, it's Dall'Aglio.'

'That was quick. Any news?'

'Not really. There wasn't an investigation as such, because there was never a crime, not that we knew of.'

'So who was Franchini?'

'How did you get his name?'

'Saw one of his adverts in *La Gazzetta*.'

'Right. He registered the boy's disappearance. It was more a bureaucratic mechanism than the beginning of

23

an investigation. That's the only thing I found, the report. Once he was reported missing some photographs will have been distributed and advertisements will have been placed in the local press. But there's nothing here in our records.'

'Who was Franchini?'

'He was one of the commanders when I arrived. Retired now.'

'No relative of Piero Franchini?' It was always worth trying to make connections. Piero Franchini was a town councillor. Had been for as long as I could remember.

'Not that I know of.'

'And what was the word on him?'

'How do you mean?'

'You know, what did they say about Franchini?'

'Franchini? A bit of a drinker.'

'Isn't everyone?'

'He was straight if that's what you mean. Straight as a Roman road. Never a hint of association with anything other than the force and his family.' Dall'Aglio was always quick to defend his uniform.

'Where can I get hold of him?'

'He moved out to the hills.'

'Anything a bit more precise . . . ?'

'Listen, Castagnetti, I shouldn't even have given you this much. You can find him easily enough. I'm not giving out addresses.'

'The village at least.'

'Medesano.'

'OK. Thanks. I owe you one.'

'You don't owe me anything. I don't trade favours

24

because they become like money. People want more and more of them. I just render public what I decide is in the public interest.'

'You're a good man,' I buttered.

'I only ask that you keep me informed of your investigation.'

'Of course.'

I drove over to Medesano. It was a town I knew a bit. A girl I used to know had friends out there.

It was a small place. There weren't many bars and only one or two were open. The first one I went into was full of early afternoon boozers. There were a few men playing cards on large, circular tables. Others were reading newspapers. The low ceiling was made up of foam squares resting on aluminium runners. A fruit machine chimed from a far corner where a wheezer was dropping his coins. The room smelt of men: aftershave and grappa, coffee and sweat.

'You know a man called Franchini?' I asked the barman.

'Sat over there.' The man pointed at a large newspaper. All I could see were fingers holding the edge of the pages.

'Small world,' I said.

'Small village,' he corrected.

I went round the side of the paper and looked at the man. He looked jowly and tired. He was one of those men who are so big they snore even when they're awake. There's something about retired cops I find melancholic.

It's as if once they leave the service their whole life is meaningless. Franchini was wearing a suit as if he couldn't face wearing anything else, but it was all creased like it was the only one he had left.

I took my coffee over. 'Colonello Franchini?'

He looked up, startled by being given his rank.

'My name's Castagnetti. I'm working on a case you left open way back.' I looked at the man's face that had dropped into a serious, defensive scowl. 'You remember Riccardo Salati?'

He almost closed his eyes and stared at me as if he resented the disturbance. 'Rings a bell.' The words came out as a single sound.

'Went missing in 1995.'

'Right,' he said unconvincingly.

'The boy was catching a train back to Rimini, you remember?'

The man was nodding slowly now. 'And he never arrived. I remember. I only remember because that woman kept hassling me for years afterwards to investigate this or that.'

'Which woman?'

'It was his mother, lived out in Sissa.'

'She won't be hassling you any more,' I said, looking at him.

'She copped it?'

'Died last week.'

'That why it's being reopened?'

'Distribution of the estate,' I said, nodding.

Franchini glazed over like he was missing his old job. 'And you've been hired to find the corpse?'

'Something like that.'

'Buy me a drink,' he growled, 'and we can talk about it.'

I lifted my chin at the barman and shouted for two grappas. The man popped the cork off a half-empty bottle and poured the water-like liquid into two shot glasses. He brought them over.

Franchini slugged it as soon as it was in front of him. I looked at him as his head went backwards. The underneath of his chin was stubbly, like he couldn't be bothered to shave properly. There were grey clumps of wiry beard poking out between the blood vessels.

He put down his glass and stared at it. 'She was obsessed by it poor woman. Anyone would be, but there was nothing I could do. He was a young lad. Early twenties. Had a woman and a kid in Romagna somewhere.'

'All news to me. I haven't seen the file.'

Franchini fixed me with a stare. 'There isn't one. He was reported missing, and that was that in those days. Nowadays they would spend all day printing off letters to relatives to keep them informed of the lack of progress. We let it drop. The way that woman went on at me, you would have thought I didn't care. I cared too much, that was what my wife always used to say.'

I nodded and let the grappa touch my upper lip. It was a powerful poison.

'I didn't ignore any leads,' Franchini looked at my glass, 'it's just that there weren't any. There was no evidence that anything untoward had happened to him. Truth told, it wasn't the first time in his life he had gone absent without leave.'

'Meaning?'

'I can't remember all the details, but that boy had a wanderer's sort of lifestyle. He played cards, lost money, borrowed money. His woman, I can't remember her name, she said something like that herself. I don't remember much more about it than that. This insistent mother and her unreliable son.'

I listened to the man slurring. He was the classic drunk, veering between the aggressive and defensive.

'So there's no file on the case?'

'All you'll find is the report listing him as missing.'

There was something about the way he said it that made me distrust him, think there was more to it than that. He had said it too nicely, and nice didn't come natural to the Colonello.

'And?' I said, making it sound like I knew there was more.

Franchini caught me looking at him with suspicion. His face was blank, but he was blinking and he gave up the pretence.

'When I retired,' he said slowly, 'I was looking forward to spending time travelling with my wife.' He paused and stared at me defiantly. 'When she died I didn't have a lot to do and I went into the same line as you for a year or two. Did a little private work to help pay the bills.'

'And you worked for Silvia Salati?'

'It was five or six years ago. Nothing came of it. There were as many blanks then as there were before. You won't find anything.' He looked at me with a drunkard's disdain, as if he were deliberately trying to give offence.

I lifted my drink again and stared at Franchini through the bottom of the shot glass. I placed the glass back on the table and signalled to the barman for another round. 'Tell me about when he went missing. Why was he catching a train?'

'To go home. Had a woman in . . . Ravenna or Rimini.'

'What was her name?'

'Emma. Or Anna. Something like that.'

'And?'

'What?'

'What was the story on her?'

'She was one of those alternative types. Living out of a caravan by the beach. That boy Riccardo had cleaned her out of money, so she had a motive. They had a pretty tempestuous relationship. Ricky put it about a bit, and she didn't hang around either. Less than a year after Ricky went missing, she had married someone else.'

'Does she still live out there?'

'Sure, last I heard. Rimini it was.'

'And their girl, what was her name?'

'I don't remember. Cute little kid. There was a stand-off as I remember between the Salati woman and Anna or Emma or whatever she was called. When I came back from Rimini that poor old Salati woman was more interested in how her granddaughter was than in the progress of the case. She hadn't been allowed near her since her son died.'

He had said 'died', and saw me notice it.

'You think he's dead?'

He nodded quickly, like it was a certainty.

'And what was the progress?' I asked, wanting to keep the drunkard on track.

'Nothing that I recall. His woman seemed like one of life's gamblers who had already written off Riccardo as a bad debt. She was moving on, that's what she said.'

I was trying to build up a picture of Riccardo's family, but it was always hard when it was through someone else's eyes, especially eyes pickled in grappa.

'And the brother? Umberto?'

Franchini squinted, trying to remember.

'He had lent the lad money too. From what people told me, Riccardo only had to open his mouth and people seemed to part with their money. He begged and borrowed to avoid calling it theft. That Umberto was pretty furious about the whole thing. He was tight as a clothes line.'

'And you think he snapped?'

'You talk to him. He says he was with his pregnant wife that night.'

'He said the same to me this morning. Why did they split?'

'I can't remember. This was years ago.'

The barman brought over more drinks and Franchini threw his back. I looked out of the window.

'And what did you make of the case?'

Franchini looked reluctant to reply. Didn't like defeat, I assumed.

'I didn't get anywhere and I was too honest to pretend to the old Salati woman that I was on the brink of a breakthrough. I told her as much but she begged me to keep looking. I had the impression she knew more than she was letting on, or that she was holding back on me. It was like she wanted me to prove something she already feared. You get a sense for these things,' he said condescendingly, looking at me through the white wire of his eyebrows, 'after forty years' detective work.'

'Was it about money?'

'Certainly looked that way. Riccardo was borrowing from one person and pretending to pay back another. It all went on gambling debts from what I could work out. He used to play the tables at the hotel out on the coast where he worked.'

'What hotel?'

'I can't remember,' Franchini said, shutting his eyes dismissively. 'I remember the older brother, Umberto, getting quite hot under the collar on the topic. Said that his brother had cleaned him out.'

'Did you check out his alibi?'

'His wife painted the same picture of domestic bliss.'

'What was she like?'

'A real ice-queen. She looked like the kind of woman who could do anything she wanted to.'

'How do you mean?'

'I don't know. You go see her. Very self-possessed and guarded.'

'Doesn't mean anything,' I said, wanting my turn at being dismissive.

More men had come in by now and the windows were steamed up against the cold. I looked back at Franchini who was cracking walnuts in his fists and piling up the shells in an ashtray.

'And there were never any sightings?'

'Of the boy?' He shook his head. 'None. I convinced myself that he was done in that night or soon after.'

'Why?'

'You get a sense for these things. You know how it is. There were plenty of people who had a grudge against him.'

'Sounds like a good time to go missing.'

'He wouldn't have been able to pull it off from what I remember. Sounded to me like he struggled to organise a tax return let alone an El Dorado one-way.'

'He could have missed his train . . .'

'I think that's exactly what happened. The train he was expecting to get was over an hour late. That was the only lead we ever had. It meant he was hanging around the station for over an hour. I think he got bored, wandered off, and never got back to the platform. But you go to the station and ask if someone remembers his face from one Saturday night fourteen years ago. All that time, and with all the chaos that's always going on there. People will laugh in your face.' The drink was making him aggressive and as he spoke the hammocks under his eyes were rocking. 'You might just as well ask a goldfish what they know about opera. Per carità!' He laughed nastily, as if I were being a nuisance.

I got up. 'OK. I'll see you around.'

'Stay for another.'

'Next time,' I said as I walked out.

Back in the car I opened the glove compartment and took out a map. It wouldn't take me long to get to La

Bassa, the lowlands. It was flat as a puddle of mud and smelt about the same.

Without this fertile land the city wouldn't survive. This is where the pork and milk come from. It's a tidy, moody place. In summer you can't move for mosquitos, and in winter you can't move for fog. The roads are thin ribbons raised up on earthy banks and flanked by irrigation ditches. If you meet a man or beast on one of these roads you need floats to let the other pass.

Everywhere there are willow and poplar plantations. They're planted in perfectly parallel lines and create enough dry earth to sink the foundations for a new house. La Bassa, Mauro says, is like Louisiana, and he should know because he saw a photograph of Louisiana once.

I always get lost around here. I confuse the small farming communities with their little, proud squares and their lonely village grandeur. I usually come out this way for some food fair or a *sagra*, one of those summer events in a field where you dance to pop music and *ballo liscio* and drink fizzy red wine out of white plastic glasses.

As I approached Sissa the road became very narrow. There were abandoned houses dotted along the road. Many windows were empty of glass, or had only triangles of it left in their frames. There were barns whose beams were giving in to the weight of age and many of the long, half-cylindrical tiles lay broken on the ground.

But then the road veered right and brought me into the centre of a picturesque village. There was a church on one side of a small square with long steps leading down towards the fountain in the middle. There was a bar on the other side of the square, and a shop. A bit further away I could see a building with an Italian flag flying next to the European one.

There was no one around. The shop and the bar and what must have been the village hall were all closed. I got out of the car and looked down all the roads that led away from the square. They didn't offer much. There was one old woman in black who was shouting for some animal or child to come indoors. In the other direction there was a man pushing a bicycle away.

I went down one of the side streets with a row of small cottages, ancient peasant houses that were shut up against the cold. The street was asphalted but there were cracks across it. I nodded a *buongiorno* at a man who was peeling potatoes over a hedge into a field of pigs.

'Know where the Salati house is?'

'Sure.' He pointed at a house where there was a cluster of shiny cars. I could see someone carrying in a tray of food. 'The end of this road,' he barked, pointing, 'the last house before the orchard. It's the one on the right where all the mourners are.'

I walked down, trying to bounce my ankle into life.

On the left was a woman in gardening gear. 'That the Salati house?' I said to her.

The woman nodded.

'You live here?'

She nodded again.

'I'm a private detective, Signora.' I let the news sink in. 'I've been employed by the executors of Signora Salati's will to verify the legal status of Riccardo Salati. Have you lived here long?'

34

'This is where I've been since I was born,' she said proudly. She pointed across the road to the house opposite. 'That's Silvia's house, the red one. She moved in the day she got married.'

'Could we take a look?'

'Not much to see. And now's not exactly a good time.'

I could see the orchard's twisted branches to the side of the Salati house. Beyond the fruit trees were vines, their thin, bare arms wrapped around long lines of wire.

'Are they going to sell it?' I asked.

'I expect so. Umberto has no interest in returning here.'

'Why not?'

'Because he's part of the provincial jet-set. Sissa isn't Portofino.'

'I prefer Sissa,' I said.

'It's a good village,' the woman said, staring at me. 'We're close knit here, and some people think that's bad. But we look after ourselves, we care for each other.'

'Including Riccardo?' I asked.

She looked at me and nodded slowly. She started talking about how her friend had continued her dignified battle for justice for her boy.

'I'm trying to work out what might have happened to him,' I said. 'I get the impression that he was unreliable . . .' I trailed off, hoping she would pick up the story, but she was pulling up a weed that had sprouted in the window frame of her house.

'He would leave on a whim,' she said eventually, 'or

35

show up on another. You never knew where he was going to be from one minute to the next. He was often away all summer working in the hotels in Rimini. Then, out of the blue, I would be woken up by him shouting to his mother in the middle of the night, asking her to open up. No warning. There was no warning to anything he did, except when he went missing. That was the one thing which, looking back, might have been expected.'

'How come?'

'Just the way he lived. Like I say, he would be here one minute, gone the next. He was a wanderer without roots, and sometimes those kind of people just', she had the weed in her hands and was looking at it, 'don't come home.'

'Did he have many friends here?'

'I wouldn't say that. But he wasn't disliked. And he certainly didn't have any enemies.' She looked over to the house opposite. 'But ever since he moved out east we all lost touch with him.'

'And who was Riccardo's woman?'

She paused. 'A girl called Anna. She came up here once or twice, but she and Silvia fell out. They were both strong women and both had their opinions.'

'What did they fall out over?'

'I don't know and I didn't ask. But I expect Silvia thought she wasn't good enough for her son and probably said as much.'

'Riccardo and Anna had a child, right?'

'They had a little girl. She was the other reason that Ricky's disappearance hit Silvia so hard. It meant she lost her little granddaughter as well.' She inhaled deeply

36

and seemed to shudder with the effort. 'Silvia mentioned them more and more towards the end. I got the impression she had an idea of what had happened. She felt guilty in some way for letting it happen.'

'Letting what happen?'

'Letting Riccardo disappear. Allowing him to walk out on his life and his family. Maybe it was just she felt guilty for giving up on him. She always said she just wanted to know. She said that until she knew she couldn't get on with her life, and she said that even as she was dying – as if she had any life left to her. I can't get on with my life until I know, she used to say.'

I frowned. I was used to these pat phrases by now. People always said the same sentences over and over, and always with such solemnity.

'She knew she was about to die', the woman was carrying on, 'and she wanted to straighten everything out.'

'How did she intend to do that?'

'Hire you, I assume.'

I nodded. 'Her other son, Umberto,' I said. 'He and his wife separated, right?'

'Yes, they're separated, but she was up here too when Silvia was dying. Roberta she's called. A nice lady.'

I tried to remember all the names I was accumulating. I didn't want to write it all down for fear of freezing the old woman. I looked at her again. She was petite. Her grey hair was pulled back into a bun so that you could see her wrinkled, elegant face.

'Did they have a happy marriage?'

'Umberto and Roberta?'

'No, Silvia and . . .'

'Paolo?' She looked at me with stern, blue eyes. She looked over my shoulder as if the distance might be able to provide her an answer. Eventually she looked back at me.

'I honestly don't know.'

'But you have an idea?'

She shook her head. 'I'm uncomfortable speculating on anyone's marriage, let alone that of a friend who isn't yet buried.'

I nodded slowly, as if in recognition of her tact. Tact, for once, was enough. It was as good as an admission that the marriage wasn't a bed of roses. Marriage never is from what I've heard.

'Were there other people?'

She shrugged and said nothing. We stood there side by side in silence for a few minutes. I've never come across the family that doesn't have secrets, and the Salati family sounded like it might have a few of its own.

'I'll go and pay my respects,' I said, bowing slightly to the woman. 'I didn't catch your name.'

'Lucentini. Maria Lucentini.'

I nodded and walked towards the Salati house. As I was going through the door, I saw Umberto.

'I thought I would come and pay my respects,' I said.

Umberto nodded and pointed me to the end of a corridor and towards the stairs. He looked different. He must have shut up the shop for *lutto* and it looked as if he had been crying. There were other women going in and out of the rooms, carrying drinks on trays. The whole house smelt of incense and spices, of cinnamon or cloves and candles.

38

I walked up the stairs and found the coffin in a room beyond the other bedrooms. It was on varnished trestles and the lid was held open at an artistic angle. I looked at her marble face. I'm so used to seeing violent deaths that it surprised me how serene she looked. No blood and no bruises. I stared at her for a minute, half expecting her to twitch back to life.

There was no one else in the room. I pushed the door slightly shut and looked around. There was a chest of drawers covered with photographs.

I looked at them all quickly and saw one of Umberto and another man from what I hoped was fifteen years ago. It must have been the two brothers, they looked so similar. Umberto already looked like he was widening out. He was simply staring at the camera. But Riccardo, if it was him, was smiling, showing a wide gap between his teeth. It was a roguish kind of face. He looked like a man who could switch on the charm like a tap.

I slipped the photograph out of its frame and into my pocket. I shook Umberto's hand on the way out, but didn't say anything. There's not much you can say when someone's dead and 'sorry' is pointless the first time, let alone the second.

I drove back to the office slowly. It was getting dark and I got lost as usual. I had turned left too soon and ended up driving through hamlets I had never heard of.

By the time I got back it was gone six. I took the photograph and ran off 200 copies on my cheap paper that warped with the warm ink. I looked at the photograph again: Riccardo's face was thinner and more melancholy in black and white. The lack of colour made him look like something from long ago, a relic from another age.

I put all my equipment in the safe: the notebook, the gun, the camera. I was about to go to bed when the phone went.

It was Mauro. He wanted to tell me a woodpecker had had a go at one of the hives and had almost made a hole. 'It looks like the thing's made of balsa once the pecker's been at it two minutes.'

Mauro was my only schoolfriend who had had less luck than me. He had gone into the army, got shot up in countries he had never heard of. Had a marriage as messy as a nightclub at dawn, only now it was a divorce, so he didn't even have that.

I kept my hives in his back garden for all sorts of reasons. Mauro didn't have neighbours, for one. And because having my stuff out there gave me an excuse to go and see him often.

'It was making an almighty noise,' Mauro said, 'almost knocking the thing over. I've shooed him away twice.'

I said I would come round. If I knew Mauro, the real reason he wanted company was to get his elbow to work.

It was only a ten-minute drive to the north of the city, and Mauro was there in his garage when I pulled in. We took a torch and went to look at the hives. He showed me the damage: a long, vertical scar. The bird hadn't quite made a hole, but he had been halfway there.

We looked at the other hives. I've only got eleven, so it didn't take long. They seemed all right. I said I would come back later in the week and fix up the cracked one.

'Drink?' Mauro said.

Mauro was like a lot of drinkers. His struggle against the poison made him into a pessimist and he ridiculed anyone who made a show of being rigorous or upright. And yet at the same time he was more idealistic than any of us, and could be brutal when he saw hypocrisy or deceit. With a glass inside him he started talking about a recent case of a well-known mafioso from down south who had been let out of prison because he had hiccups. That wasn't quite the story, but that's how Mauro told it. And from there he was quickly on to the subject of our wonderful, sad country.

'It's all screwed up, Casta,' he was saying. 'I mean, why don't people do something about organised crime? Everyone complains about the system here, but the majority has never stood up to it. A few thousand go to the piazza, but millions don't bother.'

'Mauro,' I said, 'crime is like religion: it's no good unless it's organised.'

He laughed at that, and refilled our glasses. I told him I was on a new case, and he started ridiculing me as if I had said I was taking holy orders.

'What have you got that needs redeeming?' he said, swigging his second.

'How do you mean?'

'I mean, what is it you're feeling so guilty about?'

'Maybe not doing the washing-up.' I tried to laugh. 'What do you mean?'

'I mean, why do you have to save everyone?'

'I don't.'

'It's like you're always trying to prove yourself.'

'I'm always trying to prove something. That's my job.'

'But all you're really doing is trying to prove yourself.'

'Who said that?'

'I did.'

'You're talking in riddles, Mauro. I go after real people and real crimes. Things happen, I try to uncover clues, events, motives.' I pushed away my empty glass. 'I'd better head off, I'm going to a funeral tomorrow,' I said.

Mauro slipped in his watery way from spiteful to solicitous. That's why I still liked him. He would challenge you constantly, but in the end he always cared, though he hated to show it. 'Anyone I know?'

'No. It's work.'

'Let's raise a drink to him.'

'Her. I've raised enough for today. I'll see you tomorrow.'

I glanced at old Mauro. His face looked desperate, like he couldn't stop what he was doing, which was filling up our glasses. If I didn't keep him company he would sink both, so I picked up mine and threw it back.

Tuesday

I woke up with a headache the next day. It was another morning of dense white fog and as I walked to my car I could just see the vague outlines of people shuffling along the pavement, their collars tight around their throats.

I drove back to Sissa. It was a short drive and I was there two hours before the funeral was due. I parked in the piazza and looked at the church. The wooden door was open so I walked up the steps and shuffled inside.

It was dark and still. The walls were so thick that the silence seemed to echo. The roof was supported by a row of wooden triangles that rested on thick walls where the old mortar had dried mid-drip between the bricks, forming cracks which spiders had tried to conceal with their white lace.

There was something about this blank hole of a building that seemed to echo emptiness. Perhaps that's all church was about. A hollow, meaningless building where hollow meaningless people could feel they belonged. It certainly made me feel at home.

I heard the sound of someone coughing. I listened more carefully and heard muffled footsteps from inside the vestry, to the right of the altar.

The footsteps came closer. A tall man in an ill-fitting

jacket and a dog collar marched down the little church's only aisle.

He walked past me without looking. Either he hadn't seen me or he assumed I had come in to be on my own. I looked over my shoulder and saw that he had sat down on a bench in a recess at the back of the church.

I got up and walked over. 'Is this your church?'

'One of them. They spread us thinly nowadays.'

I introduced myself but the priest didn't say anything other than '*piacere*', so I didn't get his name.

'Did you ever know a man called Riccardo Salati?' I asked. It sounded abrupt in the quiet of that building, and he looked at me sideways.

'Chi?'

'Riccardo Salati.'

The priest sighed and put his head on one side.

'I've known a lot of Riccardos,' he said.

'Ever a Riccardo Salati? He grew up here in the 1970s and 80s.'

'I only arrived in 2001.'

'So you never knew a Riccardo Salati?'

'There's a Salati, a Silvia Salati, here. Or there was. She died on Friday.'

'She was Riccardo's mother.'

'I see.'

Priests were always like this. You started trying to get information from them, but ended up getting the feeling that they had got it from you.

I looked at him. He had an unusual face and jokey, sad eyes like a puffin. And he was younger than most. If he hadn't been wearing the dog collar he would have seemed completely normal. He was completely normal, I reminded myself, as much as any of us ever are.

'Do you have records?' I asked.

'Records?'

'Births, marriages, deaths.'

'We have records for everything,' he said cheerfully. 'All services, meetings, baptisms, first communions, marriages and funerals.'

'Which are kept?'

'In the church office.'

'Can I have a look?'

'Of course.'

We stood up. The representative of Rome is always the surest way into the Italian countryside. I should have thought of it when I was here yesterday.

We went through to the vestry. Along the far wall was a low, plastic cupboard with sliding doors that didn't move smoothly.

'Each register covers a twelve-month period,' the priest said. The years were written in thick pen on the spine of each binder.

I took a handful and laid them on the table. I went through them hastily, skipping past irrelevant things like collection amounts and congregation size. There were fewer baptisms or marriages as I went on. The only thing on the increase was the funerals.

An hour later I had everything I needed. Silvia had married Paolo Salati in 1958. Umberto had been baptised in 1960. He had had his first communion with six other villagers in 1969. Riccardo was baptised in 1975 but had never had a first communion. I kept going until he got to 1980 and decided Riccardo either didn't like church, or church didn't like him.

'What are you looking for?' the young priest asked.

'Everything and nothing.'

I walked over to the plastic cupboard and pulled out two more volumes: 1994 and 1995. I leafed through everything quickly. In spring 1995 I found an entry for Paolo Salati's funeral. I wrote it down alongside the other names and dates and put the volumes back.

The priest was sitting down in a corner with a large, leather book.

'Isn't it Silvia's funeral this morning?' I said.

The priest looked up. 'Could be. But not here. I never saw her in church and she's not one of those who only come feet first, if you see what I mean. She'll probably go straight to the cemetery.'

The priest went back to his book.

'I'll see you around,' I said.

He didn't say anything but nodded with a smile.

I went back to the car and drove beyond the cemetery and turned it around so I was facing the road that the mourners would be coming up. It was still half an hour before the ceremony was due to start, so I opened *La Gazzetta* and pretended to be reading. I skimmed through the headlines. It was mostly reports about *viabilità*: how new roundabouts were replacing traffic lights and making the city move more smoothly.

It doesn't need to move more smoothly, I thought. It already has a velveteen smoothness that is thrown like a blanket over any dust or dirt. There's an official civility that makes the city blissfully polite and considerate. But it also means that people see no evil, or pretend they don't.

I put the paper on the dashboard and looked down the road. The fog was lifting slightly but the colours still looked boringly uniform: wet and white. A few minutes later the first two mourners appeared.

I picked up the camera from the passenger seat and moved the lens anticlockwise to bring them into focus. It was an old couple. Soon others were coming and I zoomed in on them, letting the shutter rattle as I took repeated snaps of their slow walk to the burial site.

I recognised Umberto Salati and Lucentini, the old woman I had spoken to yesterday. Salati was with a woman and two young boys. Some other younger children were there. But in all there were only thirty or so mourners, mostly elderly.

Once they were inside the cemetery, I checked all the photos on the screen. They were all good, clear shots. Another index to add to the list of mourners from *La Gazzetta*.

I stared out through the windscreen. Funerals always make me think of the accident, of when my parents cart-wheeled their car on the A1. It was three days before my eighth birthday. Theirs was the first funeral I had ever been to. I can't remember them any more, just their faces from the photographs. But I remember the funeral and what happened afterwards. I went off the rails like their car went off the road.

I lost not just my parents but also the idea that life was worth living. I was passed from relative to foster parent to priest. Every few months I was checked in and chucked out. None of them could handle me. I didn't want them to though plenty tried, quite literally. I spent the next half of my childhood in institutions. When you live like that you learn pretty fast who's coming to hurt you or help you. You work out pretty quickly who's telling the truth and who's bluffing. And you realise that if you're in any doubt it pays to fear the worst.

I shut my eyes and tried not to think about it.

When they came out half an hour later, they were walking differently. Umberto and his ex-wife, the woman I assumed was his ex, were holding each other's arms. Lucentini seemed stiffer. The children had stopped running and were holding on to their parents. It must have been the effect of that first fistful of earth, that thud of mud on wood. They had buried Silvia Salati.

I started the car and drove back to the city. I pulled up in Viale Mentana and looked at the familiar logo of the masthead written in slanting, metre-high letters. It was illuminated for the passing traffic: LA GAZZETTA.

There was a girl at the front desk reading something hidden on her knees.

'Where's the necrologi department?' I asked.

'Fourth,' said the girl, not looking up.

I took the lift up. On the fourth floor it opened on to another front desk.

'Necrologi?'

'Yes.' The girl said it quietly as if she was offering condolences. I figured she must be doing that all day.

'My name's Castagnetti, I'm an investigator.' It came out formally, and the girl looked up at me. I flashed my badge. 'Who is the editor of the pages of the dead? It's in connection with a murder.'

The girl stared at me like I had blood on my face. She didn't say anything but walked briskly around the open-ended wall towards the office behind. I heard phones ringing and the rattle of computer keys. Dictations to the departed, I thought. I noticed I was already talking about the disappearance as a murder. Partly because it made people sit up and listen, but mainly because that was what I felt sure it was.

A man came round and introduced himself. I didn't catch his name, but clocked his face: he looked in his thirties but his head was shaved completely, the sort of skinhead that baldies go for. There was something about him that made him look slick. Maybe it was just his shiny tie and his polished shoes, but I figured he liked a fast buck and fast women.

'Somewhere quiet we can go to talk?' I asked.

'The canteen is about as quiet as it gets.'

'Show me.'

We went down a long, narrow corridor into a small room. We sat down by a window overlooking the main road.

'How can I help?' He looked eager and curious at once.

'Say I place a notice of mourning with you, how am I charged?'

'Per word.'

'And so if I know how many lines there are in a mourning notice, you know how much I pay, right?'

'Exactly. A word costs two euros fifteen, plus VAT. A photo is forty-two fifty extra, and a cross will cost you fourteen.'

'All plus VAT?'

'Everything plus VAT.'

'Even the cross?'

He nodded.

I pulled out the photocopy of the mourning notice from Riccardo. Or rather, from the person pretending to be Riccardo. I threw it across to him and he pulled out his mobile phone and thumbed in a few numbers.

'Then I reckon you paid thirty-six euros, twelve cents.'

'Exactly?'

'I'll have to check.'

'Would there be any record that I paid that amount?'

The man stared at me. It looked as if he were readying his defence against any accusation of evasion. 'Of course there is. In our accounts we enter every transaction.'

'I'm checking up on a confidence trickster.'

The man nodded. 'I heard it was a murder.'

'Might be both.'

The man shrugged.

'This necrologio was published in Monday's edition. I'm looking for any payment for thirty-six euros and twelve cents made on Sunday. Is there any chance you could find a payment of that quantity in the transactions from the weekend?'

The man raised both his palms to me. 'There are confidentiality issues here. We don't give out those sort of details.'

I hear it every day. Everyone always says that, until I can offer them something more interesting than confidentiality.

'I didn't catch your name,' I said.

'Marco. Marco Mazzuli.'

'All right, Marco. This is what I do for a living. I look into your favourite stuff: black chronicles as you call them. You would be surprised the stuff I see. I've never really had a contact here at *La Gazzetta* . . .'

'And?' He was negotiating already.

'I'm just saying that if you help me I could help you. All I need is to see that transaction. They would never know my source. As your readers would never know yours, if you're with me.' I looked at him. Mazzuli was already imagining the scoops he could get from me, his man on the street.

'What was your name?' Mazzuli asked in a whisper.

I passed him a card.

The man was already nodding. He could see an easy bargain. He stood up. 'Stay here. This will take a while. We run hundreds every day and thirty-six euros and twelve cents isn't that uncommon.'

'So I've seen.'

The man got up to leave and I looked around the canteen. It was clean and cold. An elderly woman was shouting something out back. From the window where I was sitting I could see the traffic outside. It was almost lunchtime already and the cars were static and noisy as

53

they crawled home. The canteen began to fill up with one or two customers.

The man came back with a thick roll of narrow paper. 'This is the cashier roll for the Saturday and Sunday.'

He gave one end of the paper ribbon to me but kept hold of the centre of the roll with his thumb and fore finger. It unwound as he took a step back.

I looked at all the numbers. Every few centimetres there were transactions: the amount, method of payment, the date and the time. I scanned about a metre of the paper and saw only one transaction of thirty-six euros and twelve cents.

'How many people worked the register that day?'

'Just Suzi.'

'The girl who's on there now?'

'Right.'

'And is there any way of knowing how these were paid?'

'It says here,' the man whispered. 'Debit card.' He passed me another slip of paper. 'This is our Visa record.'

I looked at it. The slip reproduced the date, time and amount of the transaction. The card details were hidden by asterisks bar the last six numbers. There were two numbers, then a space, then another four. I wrote down all the digits.

'And do people have to come in to make a payment or can they do it over the phone?'

'They don't have to come in, just as long as the money does,' Mazzuli smiled sweetly.

'All right, thanks.' I got up to go, but Mazzuli stood up and blocked my way.

'Hey, hey. We had a deal. I pass you information, you pass me. What is this you're working on? I haven't heard of any murder.'

'Me neither. But the minute I do, you have my word, you'll be the first person I call.'

'So what's this all about?'

'The opposite of a murder, I expect. Someone's impersonating a poor guy who's died.'

'I don't get it.'

'Neither do I.'

Mazzuli seemed satisfied with my confusion and smiled. As I walked out I saw Suzi passing a chip-and-pin machine to a mourner.

For some reason I decided not to go on the motorway to Rimini, but to drive the Via Emilia. It's a strange road, so straight you could drive it with your knees. All along it are rectangular warehouses, depots and shops: furniture outlets, wholesale food suppliers, regional offices of some important acronym. They look like they're all made of thin metal. Very few of them seem to have windows but they have huge forecourts for cars. It looks strangely soulless, all cuboid compared to the stone and marble extravagance of the *centro storico*.

The city has such a bizarre contrast between its historical centre and its modern suburbs. It goes from the sublime to the functional, from narrow to wide, from cobbles to asphalt, in the space of a couple of traffic lights. I suppose every old city is like that. It's just that not many have as much history as this one, or seem so impatient to get away from it.

Fed up of traffic lights and pedestrians, I pulled on to the motorway after twenty miles. It was just as straight and boring. It ran between the Via Emilia and the new, high-speed train line between Paris and Rome. East and west, the road was the same: flat fields and crumbling villas, the occasional yard selling cranes or pallets. As the motorway cut through the outskirts of cities, I could see the tents and chickens of the gypsies and drop-outs.

I was thinking about the Anna di Pietro woman. If Riccardo was dead, she was his common-law widow. She must have given up on him long ago. She had married, Franchini had said. Their girl would be a teenager by now.

I came into Rimini on the ring road. It's a place of wasted beauty in the low season. Long beaches to yourself and the litter. It used to be the place where the stars hung out in the 1950s, but they had left as soon as it had become popular in the 60s and 70s.

By now it looks like any other seaside town that has tried to make money as quickly as possible. It looks like Miami with less beach and more concrete. The grand old hotels have been turned into seedy nightclubs or knocked down to make way for car parks.

I found her road, Via dei Caduti, and parked outside the building. I found her surname and rang the buzzer.

'Who is it?' a female voice said.

'I'm a private investigator. . .' I trailed off. It always

unnerves people and I let it sink in. 'I'm looking into Riccardo Salati's disappearance.'

'Why?'

'No one told you?'

'Told me what?'

The surprise sounded genuine.

'I would rather talk face to face.'

The line went dead and I took a step back from the *citofono*. Judging by the plush block it looked like Anna had gone up in the world. It was a long way from the caravan I had heard about. I wasn't sure she would want to think about Riccardo, let alone talk about him to a stranger.

A minute later a petite woman came out of the front door. She looked overdone: the eyelashes had thick mascara and her lacquered hair looked like it could survive a gale. I guessed there must have been a fair amount of inner turmoil for her to want such solid hair, as if it could offer a bit of stability in a fickle world. As she walked towards the gate, she glanced left and right, at the balconies of the villas next door.

'We can't talk here,' she said. 'Let's walk.'

'What's wrong with here?'

She looked irritated and lit a cigarette.

'So no one told you?' I asked.

'Told me what?' She was walking me away from her house.

'Silvia Salati died on Friday.'

She stopped walking and looked straight at me. 'I heard. Umberto called on Saturday morning. And I'm sorry,' she said formally, as if she had to prove it. 'I'm sorry to hear of anyone's death. But she never liked me, and I didn't exactly take a shine to her. She was a severe woman. Is that why you're here, because she died?'

'I'm here to find out what happened to Riccardo.'

'Who hired you?'

'She did.'

'Posthumously?'

'Right. I've got to satisfy the conditions of her will and ascertain,' I paused, realising I was already sounding like Crespi, 'what happened to Riccardo.'

'You want to find out about Ricky?' She gave a snort of derision. 'I've heard that before. Ever since he went missing I've had the police, the press, the privates. None of it has made any difference.'

'I'm sorry,' I said, like it was a condolence. That's what it was because I didn't believe Riccardo was alive. I've seen enough of these cases to know that Riccardo had died within hours or days of his disappearance. The body might be lying around, but the soul was long gone.

'Listen,' I said, giving her the '*tu*', 'I doubt we'll find Riccardo. And if we do, I doubt he'll be living. But there's an inheritance involved. I need to satisfy myself of certain facts before making recommendations to the executors of Silvia Salati's will. You with me?'

She was looking at me now as she dropped her cigarette on to the pavement and scuffed it with her shoe. 'So that's why you're here?'

'I need to ascertain his legal status,' I said.

'It's "missing". Been that way for years.'

'And why didn't you ever apply for it to be changed?

58

An absence that long is more than justification to initiate a "presumed dead" application.'

'Makes no difference to me. Either way he's not here, is he?' She was looking at me, defying me to contradict her. 'We weren't married so it's not as if I had something to gain from him being presumed dead, or presumed alive, or presumed anything.'

'It makes a difference now,' I said, holding her stare. 'There's money at stake and Elisabetta is Silvia's grand-daughter.'

She was shaking her head. 'We don't need her money.' It didn't seem like the years had chilled her anger.

'Why didn't you ever marry Riccardo?' I asked, wanting to know the gripe between her and the old Salati woman.

She pulled out another cigarette and lit up. 'You don't waste time, do you?'

'I'm coming to the party fourteen years late, I'm in a rush.'

She inhaled deeply and turned her face to blow away the smoke.

'What is it exactly that you're after?' she asked. 'Because I doubt you'll ask me anything I haven't already been asked, and I doubt I'll be able to tell you anything more than what I told everyone else every time they came round here.'

'Maybe not.'

'Every time this story comes up, it throws my whole family into embarrassment. My husband, my daughter, myself. Ricky's dead. If you can prove that I'll thank you for it, I really will. Not because I didn't love him, but

59

because you'll allow me to mourn him, and allow me to start a new life at last. Because Giovanni and I feel . . .'

'He's your new man?'

'Sure.' She took another drag on the cigarette. 'Our lives are put on pause every time Ricky is mentioned. If he were dead and buried, it would be different. I'm sorry if that sounds callous, but that's how it is.'

'I understand.'

'Maybe you do,' she said, 'maybe you don't. Maybe you just know the jargon. Closure, they call it.'

'You still haven't answered my question. Why didn't you marry Riccardo?'

She stared at me, looking like she was weighing me up. 'Why didn't I marry Ricky?' She laughed. 'Because his mother was opposed to it. She didn't want him to waste himself on a girl who lived in a caravan by the beach.'

'Silvia Salati was against it?'

'Sure.'

'You were both adults.'

'In age we were, though you wouldn't have known it. He was her little boy. She was protective in ways that confused him. She manipulated him. Going against her will had consequences. She was helping him out financially. There were all sorts of threats about what she would do if he tied himself to me.'

'She was lending him money?'

'Lend was an elastic term to Ricky. She was giving him money, sure. I didn't even want to get married, but she had made it pretty clear I was to exclude the idea anyway. I stopped going up there altogether. I hadn't seen her for two years when Ricky went missing.'

'You seem to have moved up in the world since then,' I said, casting an eye around her salubrious suburb.

'It's called middle age,' she said.

We had walked towards a small park where a grey-haired woman was pushing a young child on a swing.

'And what was he like?' I said softly when she seemed calmed.

She laughed with a wheeze.

'Ricky? He was all show, just like Umberto. Only he didn't have his luck. He was a real charmer. He could talk and talk, and make you laugh. But when he went out the room you couldn't remember a word he had said.'

'When did you meet him?'

'When I was a barmaid at the Hotel Palace.'

'The one on the waterfront?'

She nodded.

'Doing what?'

'He was working there for the summer as a lifeguard and poolside assistant. By the end of the second week Ricky was asking if he could fix drinks for the guests. Sometimes he came in wearing only flip-flops and a beach gown, like he owned the place. The manager hated him, but the guests thought he was a hoot. I think it was because he was seventeen and full of dreams. People loved his infectious confidence. We ended up visiting each other's rooms off duty and you can imagine. By the end of the summer I was pregnant. We were only together properly for a couple of years. At the Palace in the summers, at my caravan in the winters.'

'How was he earning his dough?'

'Same as before: working poolside, opening deck-chairs, fixing drinks, making friends.'

'And in winter?'

She shrugged. 'I suppose you would call him a hustler. Only he got blown around because people had more bluster than him. He was never successful in business because they always pulled something on him.'

'Like what?'

'I don't know.'

'Go on.'

'Oh, everything.' She sighed heavily. 'He tried to make fitness videos.'

'And?'

'He spent millions of lire hiring the equipment and the girls and never made a single video. I can't remember why. He invested in a company that built swimming pools that couldn't hold water. He imported sandals from an Austrian he had met in a bar. He paid two million up front and received seven of them. It wasn't even an even number. He got three pairs and an odd one.' She laughed bitterly.

'Did he have debts?'

'He didn't, the rest of us did.'

'Who?'

'Me, his mother, Umberto. He called himself a professional gambler, as if it were something to be proud of. He borrowed from his mother constantly. That was why he had gone round there that weekend, to ask for money. He borrowed from me. Usually he would tell me about some sure project that would make us wonderfully rich, if only we could get in there first and invest before anyone else. And each time he got burnt it only made him more keen to keep trying, to prove them all wrong.'

'And he borrowed from you?'

'Sure. Only he knew I was drying up. I didn't have anything left to give him, not if I wanted our child to eat. So he went after anyone who would listen to him.'

'Umberto?'

'Sure. It was the same with all of us.'

'Where did he go to lose it?'

'The same place he earned it. The Palace. He would spend more money there in a night than he could earn in a month.'

'Cards?'

She nodded.

'Scopa? Blackjack?'

'Anything. He would play anything as long as there was money involved.'

'And he ran up big losses?'

'Like I said, we did. Not him.'

'You always paid his debts?'

'I had no choice. What would you have done?'

'Doesn't seem to have made much difference. How much?'

'A few million lire.'

'How often?'

She moved the top of her head from side to side as if to say that it was a regular occurrence.

We watched the grandmother lifting the child out of the swing. Ricky sounded like the usual, unreliable rover. He had settled down with a woman only long enough to get her to open her purse. He ran around Romagna trying to spin cash out of get-rich-quick schemes. He had bad debts and worse friends. The most likely scenario was that an angry, impatient creditor had caught up with him and made him pay in the highest currency there is. It might have been his brother. It might have been this woman. It might have been another gamer from the Palace.

I looked at Anna again. There was something cold and calculating about her. I had noticed it when I had mentioned inheritance.

'Those months before Ricky went missing, anything happen?'

'How do you mean?'

'Any unusual behaviour? New friendships?'

'Unusual behaviour was all there was in Ricky's life.'

'You make him sound pretty shallow.'

'No,' she fixed me. 'No, he wasn't. He was unpredictable. He did unexpected things. If he won a lot of money he couldn't sit on it. He would have to invite everyone around, have a big party, show he wasn't a loser.'

'And that summer he went missing. 1995. Anyone new in his life?'

She looked at me with tired eyes. 'I don't suppose he was any more faithful than other men. But I didn't ask and he didn't say. I would see him getting all dressed up to go out and put two and two together. But there was nothing new about that. He had been doing that ever since I was pregnant.'

'Was he asking for money at the time?'

She closed her eyes, as if this were the first question she had thought about. 'No, no he wasn't.'

'Wasn't that unusual?'

'Yes, I suppose it was. I didn't think much about it because he was always saying that he was turning the corner, that this time it was for real. That he had everything sorted out. I didn't listen to him because I had heard it all before. I recognised that excitement in his voice. It was all self-deception. We always had more money in the summer anyway. It was the only season we had regular work at the hotel. And he was a master at soliciting tips. He didn't have time to gamble. He had even given me back some of the stuff I had lent him.'

'How did he manage to do that?'

'I don't know.'

'How much?'

'Small change. A few million lire.'

'And that day he went back to the city for San Giovanni. Where were you?'

'I was in the caravan. He left early morning, before I was even awake. I was here all weekend.'

'On your own?'

'With Elisabetta.'

'Your girl?'

'Sure.'

'Who was how old?'

'Two.'

'Not much of a witness.'

She looked at me with a sour look. 'I've been through

all this before. He got on a train that Saturday morning and I never saw him again.'

'He never came back?'

'When he wasn't home that night, I assumed he had stayed with his mother. It happened often enough.'

'He didn't call?'

'No. And I wasn't going to call her house.'

'And when did you report him missing?'

'On the Monday night. He missed a shift at the hotel. He didn't always come home, but he never missed a shift at the Palace. He was due to do the Monday night, and he didn't show. They called me and—'

'What did you do?'

'I called his mother.'

'I thought you didn't do that kind of thing.'

She stared at me through her thick eyelashes.

'What did she say?' I asked.

'That she had dropped him at the station on the Saturday night.'

Her eyes had filled up and were about to overflow. As she blinked tears fell on to her cheeks, bringing with them burnt matchsticks of mascara. 'That's when it all started. She made all manner of accusations.'

'Meaning?'

'She thought I had failed to look after him. Umberto was coming round here every other night. So was Tonin.'

'Who?'

'Some old guy. Massimo Tonin.'

'What did he want?'

'Same as all the others. Wanted to know where Ricky was.'

66

'Who was he?'

She laughed. 'Ricky used to call any new friends investors. He was probably in on some project or other. He was from one of those tiny villages near the Po. He came round here demanding to know where Ricky was.'

'When?'

'The first week after he disappeared. Made the same sort of accusations that everyone else has made, said I must have seen him, must know something.'

'Why?'

'I assume he thought I was to blame.'

'When was this?'

'Towards the end of that week. Once it had been made public that Ricky was missing. He seemed desperate to get hold of him.'

'And where will I find this Massimo Tonin?'

'He lived somewhere near the city. La Bassa I think. They had only met a few months before.'

'Come here,' I said, taking hold of her upper arm. She tried to shrug off my grip, but I tightened it and she stamped her heels. I walked her towards the car. I opened the door and pushed her into the passenger seat. 'Don't move,' I said, walking round to the boot. I pulled out the camera, switched it on and sat behind the wheel. I held the thing towards her. She looked at the images: mourners in black walking towards the cemetery.

I flicked through the photographs and she started naming them. 'There's Umberto and Roberta. The boys. I haven't seen them for years.' She took the camera in both hands and looked at the boys' faces.

'You didn't want to go to the funeral?'

'Whatever else I am, I'm not a hypocrite,' she said.

'And what about Elisabetta? Doesn't she have a right to go to her own grandmother's funeral?'

The woman looked at me and, for the first time, looked guilty. It was clear she hadn't even told her daughter yet.

I took the camera back and sped through the photographs. 'Tell me if you see Tonin.'

'Go slower.'

My thumb kept clicking the shift. People got larger on the screen as they got closer.

'That's him.'

It wasn't what I had expected. He was a tall, thin man with white hair. He had an overcoat with large shoulders, which only made his legs look thinner. The photograph showed him walking on his own. His face was a long way off, but it looked set against the world. A hard, marble face with a long, thin nose.

'You sure?'

'Absolutely.'

'Family?'

'Don't know.'

I nodded. I had to talk to Tonin. I could make an educated guess about what had been going on, but it was no more than a guess. Silvia Salati's husband had died in 1995 and suddenly another man was getting close to young Riccardo. Someone was setting him straight financially.

'How old is Elisabetta now?'

She shot a defensive stare at me, as if she wanted her daughter kept out of it. 'Fifteen.'

'And you've got other children?'

'A boy. I married a few years ago.'

'Congratulations,' I said, sounding insincere. 'When exactly?'

'A year or two after all that.' She shrugged.

'I heard it was just a year.' It might have come out more mean than I intended, because she pointed a finger at me and sneered.

'There was no overlap.'

I leaned across her to open the door. 'I'll be in touch. If you think of anything, call me.' I held out one of my cards. She took the card but didn't move. She sat there for a few seconds, thinking. She looked at me as if sizing me up. 'If you're going to drag us through all this again I implore you, for the sake of my family, do it quickly.'

I nodded and started up the engine.

The Hotel Palace was dead in winter. In the foyer two boys were playing football with a screwed-up piece of paper. Their uniforms were unbuttoned and they looked like schoolchildren in a playground. They stopped when they saw me and one of them went behind the front desk.

'Any grown-ups around?' I asked.

The boy pointed through a doorway. It led through to a windowless box of a room. A man was pulling glasses out of a cardboard box and lining them up behind the bar.

'Can I get a drink?'

The man grunted. 'What do you want?' The accent was Calabrese.

'Give me a malvasia.'

The barman grunted again as he bent down to the fridge and pulled out a bottle. As he uncorked it, he spilt some on to his knuckles. He wiped his fingers on his oily apron, then picked up the bottle again and poured the yellow fizz into a flute.

'Three euros.'

I passed him a twenty. 'Keep the change.'

The man looked at me with tired eyes. 'What are you after, Mister?'

'Call it research. I'm trying to track down a character who used to live in Rimini in the early 1990s.' I pulled out the photo. 'He used to work here. Name's Riccardo Salati. Had a woman from around here called Anna. Anna di Pietro.'

'Who are you?'

'Castagnetti. I'm an investigator.'

'What do you want?'

'I want to talk to the manager. Or preferably someone who worked here in the early 1990s.'

'The manager's not around.'

'What's his name?'

The barman made a tutting sound with his tongue as if even this much was confidential. I looked over his shoulder and read the licence granting the bar permission to sell alcohol. The name said Lo Bue.

'Is the manager Lo Bue by any chance?'

'Rings a bell.'

'How long has he been here?'

'Longer than me.'

'Far back as '95?'

'How would I know?'

'And where is he?'

'He's not around. He doesn't show much during winter.'

'And if you've got to phone him, where do you call?'

'He doesn't like to be disturbed.'

'Say someone tells you to call him,' I pulled out my pistol and placed it gently on the bar. 'What number do you dial?'

The man opened his palms and put his hands upwards. He was staring at me with scorn. I kept one hand on the gun and pulled out my phone with the other. As the man said the numbers, I punched them in. I listened to the silence of connecting satellites.

'Sì.' A voice came on.

'Lo Bue?'

'Who is this?' He was even thicker Calabrese than his heavy.

'Castagnetti. I'm a private investigator.'

'What do you want?'

'I want to talk to you about Riccardo Salati.'

He didn't say anything for a few seconds and then: 'Who gave you my number?'

'Father Christmas. So how about it? I hear he used to work for you back in the early 90s? Him and his woman, Anna di Pietro.'

'I remember him. He was the lad that went missing.'

'That's the one.'

'Come to the hotel tomorrow. Come for lunch.'

71

'Sure.' I snapped the phone shut and looked at the barman.

'What time's lunch in your part of the world?'

'Eh?'

'Never mind.' I put the ironmongery back in its holster. 'Sorry about that. I get impatient sometimes.'

The drive back was dull and I started thinking about my bees. A few months ago I had had to burn three of my hives. They were all infested with varroa. Dirty little parasitic mites. It took a couple of minutes to burn years of hard work. Theirs, not mine.

I like them because there's never any risk of me getting attached to one in particular. There are no names and no emotions. I said as much to Mauro a while back, and he laughed, and said that was why I had problems with women. But I like the bees because they are so different to humans. They believe in hard work and hierarchy, for one.

I had got into bees way back. When I was a boy and my parents had died, I went to live for a while with my uncle somewhere in the mountains outside Turin. He had a farm. One summer there was a swarm, a nasty blob of noisy bees like a furry tear-drop just able to cling to the branch. It was throbbing like a hairy heart.

A few hours later an old man arrived and dropped the swarm into a basket. There was something about the way he did it that impressed me. Maybe it was because he was French and the exoticism of the foreigner excited me. But I wanted to have that skill, to show a child that something terrifying could actually be beautiful and productive.

I forgot all about it until I found another swarm a few years back in a hollow tree up near Fornovo. I built a hive out of some old planks Mauro had and mail-ordered the rest. I had beginner's luck for a while. The first year I got twenty-eight kilos of wonderful honey. I almost doubled it the next. I was hooked. I didn't mind getting stung. No worse than a few nettles on a country walk. It cost next to nothing. You didn't need more than half a dozen tools and a box of matches.

There was something peaceful to it. Maybe because they could so punitively defend themselves, there was a pact of gentility. If they had to sting, they died. If they stung, you were sore. So you were careful and respectful. You took their honey, but you fed them in winter, you kept them free of diseases. Or I did, until last summer.

The mites were everywhere. I tried being soft and hard. I used sucrocide and then chemicals, but nothing worked. In the end, I dug a hole in the ground, chucked the lot in there, and threw a match on top.

My phone started dancing on the dashboard. I put it to my ear and heard a young girl's voice. 'This the detective?' The voice sounded soft and uncertain.

'Sure, who's this?'

'My name's Elisabetta di Pietro. You were with my mother this afternoon.'

I couldn't work out how she had my number and then remembered. 'And you found my card in her handbag?'

'Her coat pocket actually.' She laughed nervously. 'Why is my mother hiring a private detective?'

'She's not.'

'So who are you?'

'I'm looking into your,' I wasn't sure how to say it tactfully, 'into your father's disappearance.'

'You going to find my father?'

I made a non-committal noise.

'I almost hope you don't find him alive.'

'Why's that?'

'Because the thought that he's still out there and, I don't know, never wanted to see me . . .'

It made sense. If Riccardo was alive, he clearly didn't care about her. When children are treated that way, they learn to reciprocate.

'There's no evidence that he's dead,' I said.

'You mean you think he's still alive?'

'I doubt that very much. I think it's very unlikely your father is still alive. But it is possible.'

'And is my mother a suspect?'

'Everyone's a suspect.'

'Except me.' It sounded like she was smiling and I tried to imagine what she looked like.

'You were two, right?'

'Two and a bit.' She laughed at herself. 'I still say it like I'm proud of that extra bit.'

'And when did your mother meet Giovanni?'

'I don't know. They've been together as long as I can remember. 1997 I think.'

'And your uncle, Umberto. Do you see him much?'

'Hardly at all. He calls occasionally. If he's in the area he'll drop in.'

'He and your mother don't see eye to eye?'

'Umberto doesn't see eye to eye with anyone.'

'What does that mean?'

'He only sees his own reflection.'

'Says who?'

'I do. He's so vain he looks in the shop windows to check himself out. I've seen him do it.' She paused. 'I'm sorry, I can't help myself being sharp with people. I'm, it's like, I don't know whether my father's alive, whether my mother or my uncle were . . .'

'What?'

'Responsible.' There was silence down the line.

'You don't know about your grandmother, do you?'

'What?'

I waited, wondering whether the truth was a kindness or cruelty. 'She died.'

'Is that what all this is about? Nonna Silvia died? Is that it?' She sounded as if she were losing control.

'I'm sorry it's me having to tell you this. She was buried this morning.'

There was a gasp and then the line went quiet. It sounded as if the girl was beginning to cry.

'Listen, I'm driving. I shouldn't even be talking on the phone. I'm going to do what I can to find out about your father. Just let me ask you one question. Have you ever been contacted by someone out of the blue?'

'How do you mean?' I could hear her sniffing.

'Have you ever had any phone calls from a man wanting to talk to you out of the blue? Anyone ever

75

hang around outside your school or write you letters? That sort of thing?'

'No.'

'All right, never mind.'

Back in my office I took out the white phone book. There was only one Massimo Tonin. The address was in a village on the banks of the Po.

When I got there, the villa looked grand. It was set back from the road by an avenue of poplars. There was a black iron gate and an intercom in a booth off to the right.

I peered through the iron railings to the side. There was a small lodge behind the main house. I guessed that was where they kept the domestics. It was getting dark and I could just make out a man clearing leaves from a ditch.

'Hey,' I shouted at the gardener.

The man looked up.

'I'm looking for Massimo Tonin.'

He walked towards me, leaning his rake on the fence. He had a good-looking, weathered face with deep-blue eyes. He must have been in his fifties, but his bare arms looked strong and muscular. He had the rugged appearance of someone who spent most of his life outdoors.

'Who are you, Mister?'

'Castagnetti.'

'What do you want?'

'A chat with Massimo Tonin.'

The gardener came back a few minutes later.

'Ring the buzzer, Mister,' he said, 'Mr Tonin will speak to you there.' He pointed at the glass cage.

I stepped back and held the buzzer for long enough to appear rude. Eventually there was a click as someone picked up the phone from inside.

'Who is it?' said a lazy, disinterested voice.

'Castagnetti, private investigator. You Massimo Tonin?'

'I am. What do you want?'

'A chat with you.'

'We're talking aren't we?'

'This isn't how I talk,' I said, staring at the eyeball behind the glass.

'Why don't you tell me what you want to talk about.' The voice sounded distant.

'I'm investigating the disappearance of Riccardo Salati', I said, 'and I have a funny notion he was your son.'

The man didn't say anything.

'I spoke to your granddaughter this afternoon.'

Tonin again didn't say anything. I wanted to see his face, to see what his reactions were at the mention of Riccardo's daughter. He hadn't denied anything yet, which was a start.

Eventually he spoke very softly. 'You're right,' he said, 'this isn't the way to talk about this. This is a delicate matter. Can I suggest we meet in my office at eight tomorrow morning? It's in Via Farini.'

I grunted my assent and the line went dead. 'Delicate' was good. I assumed he was talking about the sex, not the disappearance.

I stared at the grill pondering whether to push the

buzzer again. I watched the gardener who had gone back to his ditch. I wandered over towards him, as close as I could get, and shouted through the railings.

'What's Mr Tonin's job?'

'What's that?' the gardener said.

'What does the big man do?'

'He's a lawyer. Retired now. Says he's retired, but still goes in most days from what I can see.'

'And you've worked with him long?'

'Thirty years.'

'Shouldn't you be retiring soon?'

'You saying I look old?' The man smiled with a boyish glint in his eye. He dropped the smile suddenly and looked at me closely. 'What's this about?'

'I'm investigating the disappearance of a boy from way back. You ever heard of Riccardo Salati?'

'Means nothing to me. Was he one of Tonin's clients?'

'You could say that.'

It was dark now and the fog was like the inside of a damp duvet. I walked back to the car and flicked on the lights. They only made everything murkier. I could barely see the ditches either side of the road and drove slowly, only glimpsing the bends by the sudden disappearance of the roads.

Back in the office I phoned Dall'Aglio to get a bit of background on Lo Bue.

'Lo Bue?' Dall'Aglio said when I gave him the name.

'Yeah, he owns a hotel out in Rimini. You ever heard of him?'

'No. But I can run some checks.'

'Do it.' I said. 'He owns a hotel called Hotel Palace. No guests for most of the year, so what he does with the space is anyone's guess.'

'Could be anything,' Dall'Aglio said wearily. 'Brothel, immigrant dive. Have you been there?'

'Went round this afternoon. No one about but a bruiser and his boys.'

'And Lo Bue's the owner?'

'I think so.'

'I'll find out.' Dall'Aglio hung up.

I looked at the phone and wondered why Dall'Aglio was being so helpful. He usually lent a hand if he could, but he pleaded busy nine times out of ten.

I got up and looked out of the window of my office. I could see the entrance to the deli. Even in this cold, the door was open and coloured plastic ribbons acted as a threshold. I guess it saved on their refrigeration costs. I could see all the tortelli and cappelletti displayed on cardboard trays in the window.

Food is the fuel of this city. It's not just the cheeses and hams, it's all the sophisticated engineering that goes with them: the bottling machines, the slicing machines, the percolating machines – all are beautifully designed in those drab buildings along the Via Emilia.

Something had been bothering me all day and I couldn't work out what it was. It's worse not knowing why, because then I start going through all the things that might be bothering me and I'm there all afternoon: staring out of the window, unable to get out of my seat because there's so much to do. I get like that sometimes.

I speed around like a maniac for a few days, and then one comes along and I can't even swing my feet out of bed.

I was still worried about that mourning notice. Assuming it wasn't genuine, it meant someone was wanting to impersonate Riccardo. That seemed a pretty strange thing to do. At best it was tasteless. It sounded to me like someone wanting to muddy the waters. But it wasn't only that that bothered me. It was the fact that the notice had gone into the paper on Monday, so it must have been paid for on the Sunday, a day before the case was reopened. If someone was trying to muddy the waters, they must have known there were waters to muddy. Whoever placed the mourning notice must have known the case was about to be reopened before I was even hired.

I managed to haul myself out of my chair and went over to Crespi's office.

'Tell me something,' I said to him when I was finally ushered into his regal presence. 'Did Umberto bring you his mother's will last weekend, when his mother was still warm?'

'No. I've had it in the company safe for a year or so. Silvia gave it to me when her last illness was getting serious. She brought it into this office and said it was to be opened as soon as she died.'

'And when did you open it?'

'On Saturday morning. I was informed of her death and followed instructions. I took her letter out of the safe and read it.'

'And did she name me personally or ask you to hire the first name out of the phone book?'

'She wanted you.'

'And who did you tell about this?'

Crespi frowned. He realised he was under polite interrogation and he didn't like it.

'Who?' I asked again, so there could be no mistake.

'I must have . . . I mentioned it to my secretary. I keep her informed of all the cases I'm dealing with.'

'She's the statue in the front office?'

'Giovanna Monti,' he said gravely, as if my description was a slur on her honour.

'You told her on Saturday the case was going to be reopened.'

He shrugged and nodded in one movement. 'She would never divulge anything that goes on in this office.'

'So who else did you mention it to?'

The man paused long enough to show that he was running a memory check. He wasn't as discreet as he made out.

'No one. Absolutely no one,' he said with certainty.

'All right, call her in.'

He looked at me with disdain and pressed an intercom on his desk. 'Signora Monti, would you mind coming in here one minute?'

He looked at me again now with defiance. The woman came in. I stood up out of politeness, but she still towered over me. She nodded in my direction, and I took it as a chance to sit down again.

'Please,' Crespi pointed at another armchair on the other side of his office. She sat on the arm, her spine as straight as a sword.

'As you know, Signora,' Crespi intoned, 'Castagnetti

here is helping us to honour the last wishes of the late Salati, Silvia, in order to establish the legal status of her son, Salati, Riccardo.'

She nodded briefly.

'He believes knowledge of his ensuing investigation preceded his commission. He is curious to know whether you, or I', he said hastily, 'might have informed anyone else of the investigation during the course of last weekend.'

She looked at me, but turned back to Crespi and answered to him.

'I . . .' She didn't say anything more than that.

'Who?' I said.

'I might have mentioned it to a friend.'

'Who?'

'Serena.'

'Who's that?'

'Works in a law firm off Via Farini.'

'The Tonin firm?'

She nodded.

'Who is this Serena? One of the lawyers?'

'Receptionist.' The woman looked across at Crespi as if to apologise. I nodded at them both as if I had won a small victory. That was one of the satisfactions of this job: showing conceited people that they weren't as perfect as they thought they were.

I was walking towards the Tonin office when the phone started ringing.

'Sì.'

'Your friend Lo Bue's a nice piece of work,' Dall'Aglio said.

'Meaning?'

'He opened up his wife with a carving knife when she said she was leaving him. He did four months for battery.'

'Four months?' I sighed. The court case usually lasts longer than the sentence in Italy.

'He's done time before that for the usual: fencing stolen goods, importing Albania's finest tobacco, that sort of thing. He's certainly been through the university of life.'

'Only problem with that university is the graduation.' Dall'Aglio laughed.

'Who's he with?' I said, serious again.

'How do you mean?'

'Has he got a big family?'

Dall'Aglio caught the inference. 'He's from Calabria, but that doesn't mean anything.'

'Means enough,' I said, and hung up. I'm not one of those people who pretend they're not prejudiced. I think everyone is prejudiced, I reckon it's impossible not to be. All our wisdom is received rather than invented. I'm willing to be proved wrong, but when a tough nut and his crew are from Calabria, I assume he's only a phone call away from the 'Ndrangheta.

When I got to the law offices, there was a girl on the front desk. She was so beautiful that I looked for longer than I needed to. She had round cheeks, big eyes and thick hair in loose curls. She wasn't wearing any jewellery or make-up, and it didn't look like she needed to.

'Can I help?' she asked as I walked up to the desk.

'Already have.'

'I'm sorry?'

'Never mind. Tonin not in?'

'No.'

'You Serena?'

She nodded.

'How long have you worked here?'

'Who are you?'

'Castagnetti. I'm an investigator. I had a little chat with old Tonin this afternoon. He said it would be OK if I asked you a couple of things.'

She looked around at the shut doors of the adjoining offices.

'The name Riccardo Salati mean anything to you?'

She looked at me and shook her head.

'How about Giovanna Monti, know her?'

'Sure, she's a friend.'

'You talk to her on Saturday?'

'I expect so, I don't remember.' She was smiling like she was more amused than worried.

'She tell you they were reopening a case from way back?'

She closed her eyes. 'Yes, I remember. She might have said something.'

'And did you tell anyone else in this office?'

'I don't talk to anyone in this office about anything other than work.'

84

'You don't like them?'

'It's not that. It's just that our relationship is professional.'

I wondered just how professional she was. She looked it all right, her blouse all buttoned up like an ice-cool receptionist. But she might have let something slip, or someone might have overheard her conversation. Either way, the arrows were pointing towards Tonin.

'What's old Tonin like?' I asked.

She looked at me like I was asking her to be unprofessional. 'He's an old-fashioned gentleman.'

'Meaning?'

'He's courteous and kind.'

'That a professional judgement?'

'It was my mother's judgement if you really want to know. She worked here for thirty years before I started. She died suddenly last year, and Massimo looked after me, offered me this job whilst I was getting myself back on my feet.'

'What about Tonin's family?'

She looked at me with suspicion, as if I was asking too many questions.

'Is he married?'

'Sure.'

'Kids?'

She nodded. 'Just one. Sandro. He's,' she paused, 'he's had his problems with stuff.'

'What sort of problems?'

'Substance abuse. He's crossed the line from can't get enough to had too much.'

'It's a short step,' I said. 'Where does he work?'

'Here often. Not that I would call it work. He's not even a qualified lawyer. He comes in to call his friends and download films and music as far as I can work out. Uses me as a secretary.'

'I can see the attraction.'

She blushed slightly, but held my stare like she wanted to play the game.

'How old is he?'

'About your age. Mid-thirties.'

'Which office does he sit in when he comes in?' I asked.

She thumbed over her shoulder behind her. I wandered over into what looked more like a box room. There was a modern computer set up there though. I began shutting the door as I was asking her questions.

'This Sandro got a woman?'

'His shirts are ironed,' she said, turning round towards me.

'What's that supposed to mean?'

'What I said. His folds are straight. I guess it's his mother. I've heard she goes into his flat every day just to make the bed. She fills up his fridge with stuff she's cooked.'

'You don't like this Sandro?'

I watched her through the half-shut door. She shrugged like she was too honest to deny it, but too kind to say it.

I shut the door of Sandro's office and kept asking her questions. 'And who was in the office on Saturday?'

'Sandro was in,' I heard her faintly now, but clearly enough. 'He normally comes in on a Saturday.'

'Just Sandro and you?'

'I think so. There would have been a few clients coming through, dropping off documents or picking them up.'

'And when this Giovanna Monti friend was telling you about this case they were reopening, who was in the room?'

'I can't remember. But I didn't even know what Giovanna was talking about, I was just listening to her chat. That's what we do on Saturday mornings because it's always quiet. We call each other and make plans for the evening. I can't even remember this Riccardo you were talking about.'

I came out of Sandro's pseudo-office having heard every word. The box room wasn't exactly soundproof. Whether it was Sandro or not, someone in the Tonin office had heard that Silvia Salati had died and that she had hired a private detective. Someone had decided to reach for some sand, as they say. Decided to throw some sand in our eyes. Sand up the joints and cogs and connections. *Insabbiatura*, they called it.

I walked out. I didn't understand anything any more. Meeting that Serena girl in Tonin's office had thrown me. I had a small breakthrough, but all I could think about were those cheeks and those dark, innocent eyes. She seemed pure, and you don't come across a lot of purity in my line. The fact that she had lost her mother made me think we might even have something in common.

I tried to get my mind back on the job. That mourning notice. There was no way it was genuine, but it intrigued me. It might just have been someone playing a prank, but it was more likely that someone was trying to pretend Riccardo was alive and well, and the only people who usually do that know the opposite is true. It was a lead and it had led me, a second time, to Tonin.

Wednesday

The sound of my phone invaded a dream. It was ringing and rattling the wood of the table beside my bed. I looked at the number but didn't recognise it.

As soon as I answered, a slurred, female voice was screeching: 'Why did you have to tell her?'

'What?' The lime-green numbers on my alarm clock said 5:53. 'Who is this?'

'I don't know why you had to tell her.'

I walked into the kitchen and listened to her voice. It must have been the woman from Rimini. 'Tell her what? That her grandmother had died?'

'It's none of your business.'

'Business is all it is to me.'

'You make money out of grief, that it?'

'Didn't look like you were doing much grieving. And she phoned me. She found my number somewhere and started asking questions. All I did was answer them. Maybe you should try doing the same.'

'And telling her that her grandmother was dead wasn't enough. You went and told her that her father might be alive.'

I rubbed my forehead. 'No, no I didn't. I said I had no evidence he was dead.'

'Same thing. You come here out of nowhere and start whispering, bringing back . . .'

'What?'

'Everything.'

'I've brought back nothing so far.' I wanted to go back to bed but the woman sounded drunk and exhausted and I wanted to hear what she would spill. I untwisted the angular hour-glass of the coffee machine and filled the bottom half with water. I spooned the brown powder into its tray and twisted the two halves back together.

'You've brought back pain and misery is what you've done. She's been up most of the night, screaming at me for being an unnatural mother.'

'There's no such thing.' I listened to the woman stammering. 'Let me guess, she's finally asleep and you're in the kitchen swimming in self-pity and any kind of grappa you can lay your hands on, right?'

''Fanculo.' She said it like she couldn't even summon up the necessary anger.

'Listen, I'm sorry if I've caused you trouble. Like I said, I answered the phone and answered her questions, that's all.'

She sighed.

'You don't get on with your daughter, do you?'

'No mother gets on with a fifteen-year-old daughter. Especially when people like you come along and start stirring things up.' There was silence down the line and I said nothing. 'I love her,' she started saying, 'and I get nothing in return. I look after her every minute of my waking life and she acts like I've wronged her somehow.

92

Said her father would never have left if I had treated him properly. She wants to prove her independence from me by throwing every insult she knows, but the moment there's a whisper her father might not be dead, she's desperate to be a little child again, to be caught up in his arms and thrown in the air.'

I heard the machine roaring the arrival of the coffee. I held the black plastic bud and lifted up the metallic lid. The last of the coffee was spitting up into the upper chamber. I switched off the gas, poured the coffee into a small cup and took it over to the window.

'You see,' she was going on, 'I can give up on Ricky. Truth told, I gave up on him years ago. I gave up on him even before he went missing. I knew he would never be around long enough to be a father and a husband. But she can't let it go. How can a little girl give up on her father?'

'There are going to be more surprises for her before this is over.'

'What's that supposed to mean?'

'It means there's not a lot your little girl can take for granted.'

'What do you mean?'

'I need to check a couple of things, but I think she might have something to gain as well as to lose. Listen, I'm in Rimini today, I'll come round.'

'I don't want you going near her.'

'That hurts.' I laughed. 'I'll see you later.' I snapped the phone shut.

I pulled up the shutters. Outside the darkness was just beginning to give way to daylight. Through the fog I could just see the street lamps clicking off one by one. There were no cars on the roads and the only noise was the incessant chirping and trilling of birds.

The steam from my coffee created tiny bubbles on the window. I began drawing a stick man. Drips colluded and ran down the pane.

I went to find some clothes. I only get dressed for two reasons: modesty and warmth. I shave my head more often than I shave my chin. I never wear a suit or a tie. I am, by the standards of this chic city, a lost cause, a visual embarrassment to myself. Here if you don't dress up every day you're a nobody. If there's not a certain sheen to your appearance which points you out as a person of importance, people forget you're there. They assume that either you've got no eye or, even worse, no wallet. So they don't notice you, or, if they do, they underestimate you, which is exactly the way I want it.

I dressed quietly and went out into the cold. I walked aimlessly. I passed a newsagent just opening up. The man was putting out the board with the day's headlines. TALKS STALLED, it said under the logo of a national newspaper. The latest round of national pay negotiations had hit the buffers and the newspaper would be full of comment about how the country was descending into crisis.

The real news was that nothing was happening. Which was what normally happened in winter. Here, everything is as regular as clockwork: the schoolchildren, the buses, the meetings, the meals. It feels like the most punctual city in Italy. There's something about

94

the way people walk: they all know where they have to be next. If dinner isn't served at the expected hour grown men think the end of the world is nigh.

I saw a couple jogging towards the Parco Ducale. Every now and then I heard the judder of a shop's metallic shutters being raised.

It was almost eight and I headed towards Tonin's office on one of the side streets off Via Farini. I was half hoping that the girl from last night would be there, but when I rang, the same male voice from yesterday spoke.

'We're on the ground floor on the left.'

The door clicked open. I wandered across the cold stone. There, on the left, stood an old man. He looked distinguished. He had a tie and a walking stick and smelt of expensive aftershave.

'Good morning,' he said formally. 'You must be Castagnetti.'

I nodded. 'You're Tonin?'

The man held the door open for me. The office was similar to Crespi's: furnished to feel luxurious. Entire walls were covered with legal reference books. He motioned for me to sit down.

'You found us all right?' he asked.

'I'm here aren't I?'

'Could I offer you a coffee?' There was steel inside his politeness, as if his politeness was nothing more than a warning that he expected deference in return. By being so overtly accommodating, he made it clear that he demanded esteem and subtlety. It was a charade that many powerful men played, a sort of conversation in code.

'I assume this is about the will?' he said, as if he were asking after my mother.

It was a strange question to ask. But that's what lawyers did. They went to the documents and the money.

'You're wanting to prove Ricky's dead?' Tonin asked again.

I nodded. I would let the man ask his questions, but I didn't like it.

'Silvia's other son,' the man went on, placing a spoon back on the saucer, 'what's he called? Umberto is it? He'll be wanting to prove Riccardo is dead. It makes sense.'

I looked at him. It wouldn't be difficult to make the man come clean, but he would need a bit of flushing.

'Listen,' I interrupted, 'I think you're in trouble either way. You withheld information.'

'Is that so?' Tonin said, amused.

'That would be the charge. A young man goes missing and you forgot to tell the police that he was your son.'

Tonin stared at me with a stony face. 'How did you find out?'

'You show up the year Silvia Salati's husband died in 1995. Ricky's flush with cash for once and no one knows how. You go round there after he goes missing. You huff and puff the way an anxious father would.'

Tonin had lost his balance. He was trying to regain it by putting his fingertips on the edge of the table but I could see his fingers shaking. He was staring into the drying brown stains on his cup.

'It's not something I've ever been ashamed of,' he said

quietly. 'I kept it secret only because Silvia wanted it that way.'

'For decorum?'

'No, for kindness. She didn't want to hurt her husband. I don't know why. He didn't seem to have the same scruples.'

'Meaning?'

He didn't say anything.

'He never found out?'

'Not that I know of.'

'And as soon as he died, you decided you wanted to play the father after all?'

He looked at me with wry amusement. 'I met Riccardo. It was completely by chance, but I met him and we got talking, and we got on.'

'You told him you were his father.'

He nodded.

'Never gave him any money?'

He looked up at me and nodded slowly.

'He told me he was in danger. He had borrowed money from the wrong sort of people.'

'And?'

'I offered to help out.'

'In what way?'

Tonin shrugged. 'I lent him some money.'

'How much?'

The pause was long enough to know that his next line was a lie. 'I can't remember.'

'How much?'

He was shaking his head. 'Eighty-five.'

I sucked in through my teeth. 'Million lire?'

Tonin nodded.

I looked at him. That was enough to kill for. More than enough. It might even be enough to kill your child for. I've seen one killed for less, much less.

'How did you give it to him?'

'Cash.'

'When?'

There was another pause. 'I can't remember.'

I put an elbow on the mantelpiece and deliberately knocked over a vase of flowers. The water and glass formed an icy lake on the floor.

'When?' I asked. The man said nothing and I nudged a framed photograph off the mantelpiece. The glass shattered on the floor.

'Stop it.' Tonin had his knuckles on his forehead and was trying to extend his fingertips upwards. 'It was the weekend he went missing.'

'Ninety-five?'

He nodded. 'It was San Giovanni.'

Tonin must have known this was relevant. Eighty-five million. The amount and the timing said it all.

I looked at the little lawyer. He seemed broken.

'Why have you never said all this before?'

Tonin was staring into space.

I couldn't understand it. In most cases people withheld to protect themselves, but Tonin had kept quiet about giving money to his own son.

I bent down and picked up the photograph that was nude now, deprived of the frame and glass that made the two subjects look romantic. 'Who are these monkeys?' I asked, throwing him the photo.

'Teresa and Sandro.'

'Who are they?'

'My family.'

'Which family is this?'

He didn't smile, but looked at me with resignation.

I suddenly felt myself losing control. I don't often lose my cool, but sometimes people like Tonin really get to me: those kind of innocent idiots that don't do anything bad, they just keep quiet so that bad people don't get into trouble.

'I should hand you over to the carabinieri right now,' I spat. 'How could you think that this had nothing to do with his disappearance? A boy that unreliable, that irregular, and you give him eighty-five million? And then he's not around any more? You sat on this like you sat on the secret of your thing with the old Salati woman.'

The lawyer had turned white.

'You make out you're as pure as your cashmere but you're like all the others. It wouldn't surprise me if you suddenly wanted your money back and leaned on him a little too hard.'

I had gone too far, and Tonin was wagging a finger. 'The only thing I ever did wrong', he hissed, 'was to make a bad marriage. That's my only fault in all this.'

'You really do think you're innocent of everything? You withhold vital evidence in a missing person investigation, and you still make out like you're a victim.'

Tonin looked up quickly at that. 'The only victim in all this is that poor boy.' He looked at me with pleading eyes. 'What are you accusing me of?' he said.

'I want to know why were you still looking for

Riccardo after he disappeared. I heard you went round to his woman's house regularly afterwards.'

'Sure. It's true.'

'Why?'

Tonin looked at me as if I were stupid. 'Because I wanted to find him. Check he was all right.'

'Why?'

'He was my son,' he shouted furiously, banging his fist on the table top.

'It wasn't a clever way of saying to the world that you had nothing to do with his disappearance? You kept going back there to prove that it wasn't you that had buried him? Or were you going round there to look for your money?'

'I'm not responsible for Ricky's disappearance.' Tonin was speaking through gritted teeth. 'I've been suspected for fourteen years of a crime I would have laid down my life to avoid.'

'And yet you've been keeping secrets all that time. Why didn't you let people know you were the boy's father?'

'Silvia forbade it. Said it was out of the question. That was a condition of having him at all. And because,' he paused, 'that would only have hurt my wife, and Silvia's family. I didn't think I needed to publicise my relationship to Riccardo to prove my innocence. I still don't.'

'Your wife didn't know?'

'She found out.'

'When?'

'After Riccardo had disappeared. I told her. I think she must have known anyway.'

'How come?'

'Women know.'

I wondered. If that was true, maybe his wife had known long before.

'There's something phoney here,' I said. 'A man who loves his son, and gives him money, doesn't keep it hushed up for so long.' I looked at the lawyer. 'And a man who has a granddaughter doesn't ignore her.'

He looked up eagerly at that.

'You've met her?'

'I've spoken to her, sure.'

Tonin shut his eyes as if trying to picture her.

'Listen,' I said, trying to reach him, 'it doesn't seem to me like you're the kind of man who would kill his son. Only thing is, you don't seem like the kind of man to have a son, if you don't mind my saying. Until you drop the respectable, suited lawyer act and start talking to me like a man, I can't do anything for you.'

I got up and made for the door. Tonin just pushed himself up on his walking stick and nodded at me as I turned the handle.

I still couldn't understand what Tonin was keeping to himself. He seemed impassioned when accused of hurting the boy, but was shifty when I had tried to press him for an explanation of his conduct. Maybe he was simply from the old school where discretion and appearances were paramount. He had kept a secret, he said, out of kindness. It sounded phoney to me, but kindness and love always sound phoney to me. Love is normally only the afterburn of remorse.

*

I walked to the station. It was crowded with the usual suspects: salesmen and students going to Milan, groups of North Africans in sandy jackets; rounder, darker Africans with more colourful clothes and tall, elderly tourists looking at maps.

The boards announcing the reconstruction work in this square were decorated with all the most important symbols of the city: a bank's crest, the seal of the town council, the arms of a construction firm.

I looked around. There was a bar opposite where I could have a drink whilst watching the anxious commuters. I ordered a *pompari*: a twist of pompelmo with a shot of campari.

I took my drink to the fruit machine and put in a coin. I pressed some buttons idly and looked around. The station square was being revamped, the whole area to the north was being given a face-lift. The workers gathered in this bar to eat large sandwiches and drink pints of icy water. The usual customers, the Romanian and Moroccan plasterers, were talking about the worst foremen in the city.

Bicycles and pedestrians and pushchairs were going in all directions. This was rush hour. The cars were backed up as far as I could see. I recognised many of the people. That was the thing about this city. No matter how often I hear it, it still amazes me how small it is.

I found the stationmaster in his office on the second floor. He was an elderly man, short and sprightly. He was wearing the green and purple outfit with the FS logo of Ferrovie dello Stato on his chest. He had a baseball cap on his head which, given his age and the weather, seemed incongruous.

'I'm a private investigator,' I said, holding out my badge.

The man took it from my hands and looked at it closely. Officially stamped documents have an alchemic quality in Italy, and the stationmaster bowed slightly, a gesture which meant he would be happy to help.

'Taxes?' He asked.

'Murder.'

He shrugged and smiled. 'I haven't killed anything other than rabbits.'

'You know the timetables from 1995?'

The man looked at me smugly and smiled. 'Test me.'

'A train to Rimini, San Giovanni, 1995. A Saturday night.'

The man looked at the ceiling.

'1995? They had already started cutting out the trundlers. Those ones that stopped at all the villages. There would have been, let me see, the 18.32, the 20.32 and the 22.32.'

'And through the night?'

The man looked at me seriously, like he didn't like being pushed. 'Well now. There would have been something around two, and another around five.'

I looked at the old man. 'Your memory seems all right.' I was trying to wean out the man's jovial side. 'How come you remember all these timetables?'

'It was my work,' he said, pleased I had finally asked the question he wanted; 'it's what I've done every day of my working life for forty-two years. People like you coming up to me, asking me impatient questions about this or that train to this or that town. My whole life has been remembering hours and minutes and connections.'

'Snap,' I said. 'And the waiting room hasn't always been where it is now, right?'

The man laughed. 'It's moved more times than I can remember. They move it every year. In 1995 it would have still been next to the bar, on platform one.'

I was looking into the distance. 'Say someone missed a train, or the train was late, where would a young man go and wait?'

The man raised his eyebrows. 'Depends what kind of young man.'

'This one was unpredictable from what I hear. Probably prey to the usual vices.'

It was the first time the man had paused and let a question sink in. 'Some men would wait around in the parks outside. There were always a lot of people to pass the time of day with, if you see what I mean.'

'No, I don't see.'

The man looked uncomfortable. 'There were women. And boys.'

'And where would they go?'

'Parco Ducale, Via Palermo. One or two had flats nearby.'

'And there are always people selling shit in the shadows I assume?'

'Never used to be. When I started back in the 60s, we didn't know what drugs were. Nowadays,' the man was getting worked up, 'you see them hanging out there all day and all night, constantly selling stuff to young kids. There are half a dozen people within fifty metres of this office who are here selling drugs every day and the police never pick them up. Why is that? I've never understood it. They're allowed to sell poison to our children in the broad daylight. Just don't understand it.'

'Me neither.' I shook my head with what I hoped was enough indignation to persuade the man I was on his side. 'And if someone just waited in the station? Where would someone go to kill time?'

'There's the bar.'

'Which one?'

'There's the station bar. Or that other one outside the station, the other side of the bus-stops.'

I nodded. It was going nowhere. 'Listen,' I said, 'you must have seen a lot in forty-two years. A lot of people coming and going. Did you ever see anything that you had to take to the police?'

He smiled whilst blinking slowly. 'All the time. Every week I see couples screaming at each other. There are knife fights and the Ultras and political extremists. You see them all when you work here.'

'But you never saw anything, back in the summer of '95?'

'I don't understand what you mean.'

'This man.' I pulled the mug-shot from my pocket. 'He disappeared from this station in 1995.'

The man took the photo from my hand and held it up to the light. 'I know the face, I'm sure.'

'That's because it was in the papers back then.'

'That's right.' He squinted at the photograph again. 'I don't remember ever seeing him around the station, but there was some policeman who came and asked me all about it. The times of the trains and so on, just as you are.'

'Colonello Franchini?'

'I don't remember his name. We went for a drink after work—'

'That was Franchini.'

'He asked me about the trains, showed me some photographs.'

'Photographs of who?'

'He didn't say anything except they were suspects and had I seen them one particular Saturday night.'

I pulled out the photograph I had knocked off Tonin's mantelpiece.

'He show you either of these two?'

He looked very briefly, but looked at me with tiredness. 'This was many, many years ago. I see thousands of faces every day. I see millions in a year . . .'

It was useless. I would have to ask Franchini if he had ever got this far, whether he had ever got as far as the Tonin link.

I decided to take the train back to Rimini. I had a box of photocopies of Riccardo and walked up and down the train distributing them.

The carriages had corridors down one side with little rooms of six seats off to the other. My arm was soon tired from having to yank the doors open, leaning away from the handle to pull with my chest as well as my arm.

In each I handed out the photocopies. People either looked at young Riccardo's face in silence or else started asking too many questions. There was no middle ground. I answered them all patiently, telling them what little I knew.

'I remember reading about this. I can't believe it was fourteen years ago, it feels like three.'

'That so?' I said and let another door suck itself shut.

I had walked up and down the train before it even pulled into Modena. I changed at Bologna, but the connecting train was late. I sat on the platform wondering what percentage of trains were late. When I finally got into Rimini it was already past midday. As soon as I stepped out of the station the air smelt of seaweed and salt. There were fat gulls swooping on to the pavements to take any spare crumbs that the pedestrians left in their wake.

I walked over to Via dei Caduti. The di Pietro woman clicked the gate open after a little protest about wanting to be left alone. I walked up the short path towards the front door of her block of flats. She was on the third floor, a door half-ajar at her back.

'What is it now?'

'I wanted to ask you a couple more questions. Has anyone ever tried to contact Elisabetta, someone claiming to be a relative?'

She shook her head.

'No one? No calls or letters out of the blue . . . ?'

'You think Ricky has tried to contact her?'

'No, not Ricky. I fear the only person he's talking to now is his maker. I was thinking about someone from a different generation. Her paternal grandfather.'

'Ricky's father?'

'Exactly.'

'But he died in 1995.'

'Massimo Tonin was Ricky's father.'

She looked at me as if it were a wind-up. 'Are you sure?'

'Never sure about anything. But he didn't deny it this morning.'

She stared blankly over my shoulder and considered the implications. I guessed that her first thought would be dismay that there might exist yet another man to destabilise her daughter. But when she spoke she seemed only piqued by the hypocrisy of the Salati woman. Her lips were pursed.

'So all that time she was criticising the way we were living, she was lying to all and sundry. She must have known this might have something to do with Ricky's disappearance, and yet she never . . .' She looked into the distance and then stared at me. 'You're sure about this?'

I nodded.

'Nothing surprises me any more,' she said dreamily. 'All the stability we construct around ourselves collapses sooner or later. I've had so much collapse that I don't bother trying to construct anything any more.'

Except your hair, I thought to myself. 'You said Tonin came round here looking for Ricky that week after he disappeared . . .'

She nodded.

'What happened exactly? He came round to your caravan?'

'Sure.'

'And did he go inside?'

She shut her eyes. 'I can't possibly remember.'

'Think about it. It's important.'

She shook her head and looked at me. 'I don't think so. I don't know.' Witnesses were unreliable at the best of times, but fourteen years later they're as good as useless.

'Did you ever get the impression he was looking for anything other than Riccardo?'

She shook her head and frowned, not sure what I was implying.

'Is Elisabetta in?' I asked.

'I'm not going to allow you to slip a hand grenade like this into her life. She's unstable enough as it is right now. She's barely recovered from what happened yesterday.' She tried to stare at me with anger, but it was all burned out now. 'I think she's mourning her grandmother and her father and her childhood all at once, and this would only confuse her further. Let her sleep.'

The phone started ringing inside and she held up a finger and went in to answer it. I followed her into her flat and whilst she was still talking on the phone I started opening the doors. I found the girl in a small bedroom with the blinds down. She was propped up on pillows and was staring at the ceiling.

'Elisabetta?' I said quietly. 'It's Castagnetti. We spoke on the phone yesterday.'

She moved her eyes rather than her head to look at me.

'Your mother seems to think I'm to blame for upsetting you yesterday.'

'My mother', she said with her eyes shut, 'will always blame anyone except herself.'

'Oh yeah?'

'She thought I had got overexcited by the thought of. . . you know, the thought that you were going to find my father.'

'I told you, I don't think he's still alive.'

'Yeah,' she said like she was high and couldn't care less, 'I know.'

I felt sorry for her, but I didn't want to be accused of building up her hopes. Ricky was dead, I felt sure.

'I don't think he's alive. But I'll try to find out what happened.' It was my standard speech. It was what the bereaved normally wanted most. If they couldn't have their loved one back, alive and well, they wanted to know, that was all. They yearned for what they most feared. They wanted, just once, to see the kill, because it couldn't possibly be worse than what they had imagined.

'You need some sleep. I'll be back again one day when you're better and we can talk about what's come up.'

She just nodded and followed me out with her eyes.

As I was walking down the corridor it struck me that I couldn't understand how a man could resist contacting his granddaughter. Surely he would want to write to her, arrange to see her, try to claim her as his own whatever the consequences. It didn't seem natural to me. Tonin appeared to be a pretty cold-blooded customer, and it was true that he had kept his distance from his son all those years. But there didn't seem any good reason not to reach out to a granddaughter, especially since his wife knew everything anyway. It didn't make sense to me.

I was still in the narrow corridor when the di Pietro woman came back. 'What are you doing in here?' She took me by my collar and dragged me to the door. She pushed me towards the stairs and waved me away. 'Leave her alone. Can't you understand? I'm trying to look after her.'

I waved her goodbye with over-zealous politeness and walked down the steps.

I could understand her. Protecting a girl made more sense than ignoring her, that was for sure. If it was really the girl she was protecting. My mind started going paranoid. I began to wonder why she wouldn't want me to talk to her daughter. It hardly seemed like little Elisabetta could be a threat to anyone. A toddler can't keep a secret. That was Tonin's speciality.

As soon as I walked into the hotel it felt wrong. Almost all the lights were off and there was no one at the front desk. I walked through to the bar, but it was empty.

'Lo Bue?' I asked to the empty room. I was just reaching under my arm for the rod when I was smacked across the shoulders by a metal pole. My cheek caught the corner of a glass table as I went down.

A couple of kicks were aimed at my stomach and head. I put my hands up to protect my face and I rolled over into a ball, but the kicks kept coming against my spine.

'Basta.' The voice sounded mean, but it came as a relief.

I looked up through the warm blood which was dripping off my eyebrow. The fat barman from yesterday was retreating, sweating slightly after the effort of his little game of football.

The man who had called time put his face in mine. 'Don't ever come into my joint and wave a pistol at my staff.' It was the Calabrian I had spoken to on the phone yesterday.

'This the welcome you always offer your guests?' I said, spitting out some blood.

'The hotel is closed.'

'I can see why.'

Fatso stepped forward wanting to go again, but the short one held out his hand and knelt down near my face. He pulled back my head by taking a fistful of hair. 'You know who I am?'

'Lo Bue, the manager of this shit-hole?' I tried to sound casual.

'Very good.' The man smiled. His teeth appeared bright and expensive, out of keeping with the rest of his ugly face. He looked like an up-ended anvil: a thick nose on a narrow head. 'My barman tells me you were here yesterday playing the tough guy. You were lucky he didn't kill you.' The man let go of my hair and my head smacked on to the floor.

'What do you know about Ricky Salati?' Lo Bue asked.

'Ricky Salati?' I repeated, trying to work out what

was going on. 'I told your heavy back there. He went missing in 1995. That's all I know.' I glanced up at Lo Bue. He looked more greedy than guilty.

'Why are you interested?' I asked him.

The man slapped me with the palm of his hand. It felt almost soft after the toe-caps I had taken already.

'I was asking what you want. Why are you poking around now, asking questions? What's the idea?' The man put his face real close. I could smell whisky and mint. His skin was saggy and tired, even as he grimaced. 'What's it to you? What are you doing exactly?'

'Trying to find out what happened to the boy. No one's seen him for fourteen years. His mother's died. There's an estate.' The man nodded and I took my chance: 'You seem almost happy I came along.'

The man leaned forward and hit me with a backhand. I poked my tongue into a new hole on my lower lip and tasted the blood: it tasted like chestnuts.

'I don't think you know who I am,' Lo Bue said. 'What makes me happy is seeing debts paid and, if that's not possible, punishing the debtors.'

I tried to look at him, but I couldn't focus. Objects were blurring and swimming in front of me. I could feel the blood inside the bone above my ear throbbing and I couldn't understand what the man was saying. But I felt on instinct that Lo Bue needed something. If he was holding a winning hand, he wouldn't have invited me over for lunch.

I tried to figure out what was going on. Someone who had been involved in Ricky's murder would hardly start playing the tough nut with an investigator. This felt more like Lo Bue wanted to find the boy, rather than bury him.

'So Salati had debts with you?' I slurred.

'You're quick,' the man said. 'The boy left a lot of debts around here. That', he said with incongruous politeness, 'is why I would like to know where he is. And if he isn't alive, I would like to know what happened to our money. Clear?'

'I don't suppose any of you have any evidence of these debts?'

The man's face seemed to sag further as he looked at me with tired disdain. 'Don't insult me.'

I flinched, expecting another blow, but nothing came. I tried to sit up, using my left arm to push myself up against the table.

'What's the figure?'

'One hundred and twelve million lire.' It sounded precise, as if the man had carried it around with him like a bad memory for years. 'You want it in euros?'

I shook my head. I still count in lire. Always will probably. There was something about those zeros that made me feel better, like I was a wealthy man. Back in those days the lire had so many zeros we were all millionaires. Seems a long time ago now.

'How did it happen?' I slurred. My lips weren't working properly any more.

'What?'

'How did he run up the debt?'

The man looked at me like he hadn't expected to answer questions.

'A straight game of scopa,' he said quickly, as if he

didn't want to linger on a sore subject. 'It happened every night. This one was the usual. The stakes were high and they were playing quick. I had nothing to do with the tables. I just served them. It was my joint. They came here to play. But I saw it all. He lost everything at one sitting.'

'You let your staff play cards with your guests?' I asked.

'He was free to do what he wanted when he was off-duty. Listen,' the man leaned close to me again, 'don't you worry about how I run my hotel. You just worry about finding out what happened to him, and remember that I'm interested in finding out what happened to our money.'

'Oh that.' I sneered. 'I'm afraid that probably died with him.'

'That's where you're wrong. He was about to pay back. He had phoned me to arrange a meeting, said he was bringing round half of it that night he disappeared. He was about to settle.' He said it again, trying to convince himself.

'Debtors always say that.'

Lo Bue looked at me differently, with a trace of respect. 'Yeah. But this time it was real. He said he had half of it.'

'And why did you believe him?'

'I knew him. He had worked here for two years. Trust me, he was on his way here to pay back. Someone got wind of it.'

'You don't think he found El Dorado?'

'Ricky do a runner?' He coughed a guffaw. 'No.

Someone got to him. Someone who knew he was flush.'

'Like your stooge over there?' I looked at the barman. I pulled myself to my feet, but the effort made my head throb more and I felt dizzy. It felt like we were on a ship. I didn't want to show the pain, but closed my eyes to regain concentration.

'You find any information', I heard Lo Bue's voice, 'on what happened to him, you call me, clear?'

I nodded, and the barman stepped forward and pushed me towards the foyer so hard that I fell over.

Once I got outside the pedestrians stared at me. I caught sight of myself in a shop window and barely recognised what I saw.

I limped towards the station to get a train back to the city.

People kept looking at me all the way. One woman even asked if I wanted her to call a doctor.

When the train pulled in, I decided to head back towards Salati Fashions.

Salati's shop was open. It was the day after the funeral, but the girl was in there serving customers.

'Salati not around?' I asked her.

She thumbed over her shoulder and I walked out back. Salati was sitting in a small kitchenette, staring into space.

I coughed quietly and he glanced up. 'You again?' He looked me over. 'What happened to you?'

'Perks of the job. Listen, something's come up.'

'What?'

'Paternity.'

'Meaning?'

'Your father died in 1995, the year that Ricky went missing.'

'I know. It meant my mother lost both husband and son in the same year.'

'Happy marriage was it?'

Umberto looked up at me with wet eyes. 'What?'

'It just seems a coincidence. And in my trade coincidences don't exist.'

'What are you suggesting?'

'Just asking if you think it's a coincidence?'

'I don't understand what you're talking about.' Salati was getting angry. He didn't like hints that he couldn't understand. He obviously thought his mother was as pure as the driven snow.

'Let me tell you what I know. Your mother had an affair with a man called Massimo Tonin. Your younger brother, Riccardo, was their child. For as long as your father was alive, Tonin kept his distance. But in the spring of 1995, after your father had died, they started getting close.'

Salati stood up and stared at me with an icy look. Then he started laughing, but the chortles became shorter and more nervous. Then his face dropped and he looked furious. 'You don't believe that do you?'

'I do. And it's easy enough to check nowadays. A strand of your niece's hair would prove it.'

He looked at me with indignation. 'You didn't know my mother.'

'No, I didn't. Maybe neither did you.'

Salati clenched his fist and threw it at me. It came so slow that I moved to the left and pulled my right as hard as I could into Salati's soft middle. I heard Salati's breath leave him and he fell to the floor.

'Get up.' I offered him a hand.

Salati was on one knee, trying to breathe slowly.

'What,' he gasped for breath, 'did you do that for?'

'You were about to do it to me. Now listen.' I got a hand under his armpit and pulled him to his feet. 'I didn't know your mother, I didn't know your father or your brother. Chances are I never will. I'm sorry, but that's the way it is. You don't have to defend their honour because the dead don't care. You with me?'

I dropped him into a chair.

'Why didn't you tell me you had lent your brother money?'

'Because you would immediately have thought it was a motive instead of an act of pity.'

'Pity?'

'He was pitiful, believe me. He came to me saying he could no longer support his own family. He told me he had borrowed money from people who wanted it back and he had nowhere else to go.'

'I heard he went quite a few places.'

'Yeah, that's what we heard afterwards. He had borrowed from Anna, from me, from my mother.'

'I heard you were angry he didn't pay you back.'

'Of course I was. Especially when I found out he was borrowing from Mamma as well. He was leeching money from anyone who had it. He was probably richer than any of us.'

'You might have a point.'

'How do you mean?'

'Never mind.'

He stared at me trying to work out what I meant. Suddenly he started nodding slowly like he got it. I had set something off and Umberto stood up and started pacing the little kitchen area as if something had clicked. There were long, narrow boxes piled high on a table and he took a swipe at the lot, sending cardboard and silk flying through the air. He was all charged up and had a fierce look in his eyes.

'He always knew where to get money,' he was muttering to himself.

'You all right?' I said.

He just stared at me: 'Get out,' he said slowly, 'get out.'

I stood in an empty doorway and watched the shop for a few minutes. Umberto seemed alarmed by the news. If, that is, it really was news to him. It would call into question the character of his mother, just as he was mourning her. It was a hard hit to take, and Salati was the sort to hit back.

I decided to tail him. I went inside the bank opposite the shop. I punched a button for a ticket and sat down in the chairs with the other customers waiting for their number to come up. Through the window I could see Salati Fashions. Laura was in the shop folding shirts and putting them inside open boxes.

Within minutes Umberto marched out pulling on his

jacket. I watched him head towards the piazza and followed him up Via Farini. He walked up as far as Solferino and turned left into Via Pestalozzi. Salati held his keys towards a black jeep and both indicators flashed.

I ran towards the *cittadella* and whistled for one of the taxis by the entrance. One of the white cars drove up and I jumped in.

'You see the black jeep, follow it.'

'Where are we going?'

'Don't know.'

'This could be expensive.'

'I've got the money. Just don't lose the jeep.'

The taxi nestled into the traffic a couple of cars behind Salati. He pulled into Passo Buole and on to the Stradone. The four-laner was blocked by impatient, pushy traffic and we were already a few cars behind him by the time we passed the Petitot and the football stadium.

We followed him on to Via Mantova at the next big roundabout. By now the taxi was far behind, struggling to keep up as Salati's car disappeared. This was the road to Tonin's house, I thought to myself as my back was pressed into the cushioned seat.

The taxi got stuck behind some Austrian HGV and lost his chance to overtake. He pulled out to try and see Salati, but the on-coming traffic forced him back.

By now Salati must have been far ahead. I knew the left turn to the Tonin place was coming up in a kilometre or two, and took a gamble. I told the taxi to turn left by the bridge. We were outside the Tonin estate within a few minutes. I told him to slow down just beyond the gates and got out. I walked back to the gate and peered through the railings. I could see Salati's black beast parked under the central cedar that formed an umbrella over the circular drive.

I moved away and waited. I assumed Salati was in there, spitting blood. It was strange he had chosen to come here rather than Tonin's office in the middle of the city. Maybe he hadn't wanted to see the old man, I thought. It was possible that he was here to see someone else.

I saw Salati come out five minutes later. He was shouting something as the door closed behind him. He got into his car and revved the engine aggressively as he sped off. As the gates opened, I headed back to the taxi but by the time the driver had put out his cigarette, Salati would have been on the *tangenziale*.

'Forget it,' I said to the driver. 'We'll stay here.' I walked back towards the gate. I wasn't holding many cards, but surprise was always useful. I rang the buzzer.

A woman's voice: 'I told you, you're getting nothing from us.'

'Was Umberto Salati after money?'

There was silence.

'Who is this?'

'Castagnetti.'

'Who?'

'I'm an investigator.'

'What do you want?'

'I wouldn't mind coming in.'

There was silence again.

'What do you want?' she said again.

'I was wondering why Umberto Salati just paid you a flying visit.'

There was a crackle and the line went dead. I buzzed again but there was no reply. I stared at the grey gate. It was simultaneously ornate and brutal. Wealth's lack of taste always surprises me.

The air seemed solid with its freezing fog. It was thickening as the air got colder. I heard the rattle of the delivery vans back on the main road. It was an isolated, melancholy place.

I pulled out my notebook and wrote down the date and the times that Salati had arrived at and left the Tonin estate.

I was looking at the notes when I heard a car slowing down. I looked up and could see the no-nonsense rectangles of Volvo headlights.

Tonin got out. 'What are you doing hanging around outside my house?'

'Still looking for answers.'

The man stared at me with veiled anger.

'I'm interested as to why Umberto Salati should be visiting your house whilst you're away.'

The man growled, but I could tell he was surprised.

'You got any ideas?'

'What do you want from me? I've told you everything I know.'

'Have you?'

The old man just stared at me. He was wearing a black overcoat with a fur trim on the collar. He looked tired and tense. The situation was out of his control and he seemed to know it.

'What happened to your face?' he asked.

I ignored him. 'What did Salati want with your wife?'

Tonin shook his head. 'I don't know.'

'I told him that you and his mother were lovers. He didn't take it well.'

Tonin was shaking his head vigorously. 'That wasn't wise.'

'Why not?'

'Have you no mercy? Silvia was buried yesterday and already today you're telling her son . . .'

He had a point, but I didn't have time for sensitive types.

'I just spoke to your wife.'

'When?'

'Just now, on the intercom. Not a talkative type is she?'

Tonin looked confused, as if he couldn't work it out himself. He looked like he was thinking deeply himself and couldn't find an answer.

He pointed at his car, indicating to me that I should get in. I held up a finger to my taxi driver, suggesting I would only be a minute.

Tonin opened the gate with a remote and revved angrily as it swung open. As he got to the front of the house he braked hard and I heard the gravel smacking the underneath of the car.

The woman was on the phone when we went in. The hall was all marble and terracotta and her voice echoed off all the walls. She was short and slim with hair halfway between blonde and grey. She was wearing a skirt that was shorter than you would expect from someone her age, and it made her look much younger than her husband. From her appearance I guessed she read the fashion magazines, like she still wanted to look good for someone.

She turned round on hearing us and put a palm over the phone: 'Who's this?' She glanced at her husband.

'A private detective.'

'You've been hanging around outside my house all this time?' She took her palm away from the phone. 'I'll call you back.'

She looked me up and down. 'You look like a boxer who lost every round. What do you want?'

'Would you prefer to talk in private?' I asked gently.

She laughed at the question and its tone.

'I've been commissioned', I said slowly, 'by the estate of Silvia Salati to classify the legal status of her son, Riccardo.'

She shot her husband a look that he avoided.

'I believe you knew Riccardo Salati was your husband's son?'

She was still staring at her husband. 'Is that right?' There were years of resentment in her voice.

'Why did Umberto Salati come here just now?'

She didn't have a quick reply and both Tonin and I could see it.

'He said he wanted to know if it was true. Said how we were to blame for what had happened to his family.'

'What did he mean?'

'That he knew our little secret. He kept saying it.'

'Meaning?' I looked at Tonin. His eyes were closed.

'He had only just found out about,' she paused,

'about his brother. He seemed to blame my family for what had happened to the boy.'

She had recovered her composure and was talking fluently again. I had lost my chance to catch whatever it was that she was being evasive about. I looked at her face. She had a small, tight mouth which made her look mean.

'Who do you think killed Riccardo?' I asked her.

'How should I know? All I knew about him was that he was a bad one. The kind that ran up debts and couldn't stay still. It happens to some people. Especially those without a stable family life.' She looked at her husband archly.

'You didn't like him much, did you?'

'I didn't dislike him. I wanted nothing to do with him. I'm sure you can understand why.'

'Did Umberto ask you for money?'

'He said he was owed, and he was going to get what was owing to him. That's what he said.'

'And what did he mean by that?'

'That his father's fortune shouldn't be wasted on illegitimate ghosts. He said he needed proof that the boy was dead.'

'And he thought he could get it from you?'

She stopped to draw breath, exhaled dismissively through her nostrils, and sneered. 'I don't know anything about his disappearance, let alone his death. I don't know anything about his life. All I know about him is . . .'

'How he was conceived.' I finished her sentence for her.

'I'll open the gate for you on your way out.' She said walking towards the door and holding it open.

I looked at her again. Her nails were painted a dark red, the same colour as her thin lips.

I bowed towards Tonin, feeling cowardly for leaving the poor man alone with such a woman.

As I walked back along the gravel, my footsteps sounded loud. I turned to look at the house, but the front lights had been switched off and it was in darkness. Someone must have been watching though because the gates swung open as I approached them.

As they closed behind me I stopped. I looked at the buzzer and walked towards it one last time. I pushed the button and held it. No one answered. I had wanted to know how many children they had, how many children of their own. I made a mental note to find out.

The taxi driver was impatient when I returned. We headed back to the city in silence. I was thinking about what I had heard. The woman seemed to know all about Riccardo. She had the weary, sarcastic tone of the wronged woman who didn't want to be reminded of a past humiliation or slight. She must have been able to see what was coming. Umberto Salati had felt so indignant that he decided to confront the Tonin family, to insist that they compensate him for anything they had done wrong. I wondered what that was. What, other than dishonouring his father, did he blame them for?

I looked at the fields in the dark.

'You been in this business long?' I asked the driver.

'Twenty-odd years. Since I left school.'

'Always hanging around the station?'

'Station, stadium, schools. You never know where you're going to end up. That's why I like it.'

The car was speeding back towards the *tangenziale*.

'You the longest serving in that line-up?'

'Just about. There's a couple been there longer than me. But apart from them, I'm the veteran.' He laughed.

Within a minute or two, we were approaching the outskirts of the city. There were static cranes and unfinished housing blocks amidst the frozen mud.

'What's the furthest anyone's ever gone with you?' I asked.

The man chuckled to himself. 'I used to have a good number driving an Austrian girl to Vienna and back. Lovely girl, an Erasmus student.'

'Ever take anyone to Rimini?'

'Couple of times, sure. In the summer.'

'In 1995?'

The driver put his brakes on gently and the car slowed down into the darkness.

'What is this?' he said quietly, catching my eye in his mirror. 'If someone wants to ask me a question, I prefer they do it straight, if I explain myself.'

'Try this: you ever heard of a boy called Riccardo Salati?'

'Yeah, sounds familiar. Who is he?'

'Was he. He went missing in 1995 whilst waiting for a train to Rimini.'

The man was nodding slowly like it was all coming back to him. I looked at his ID on the dashboard and memorised the number just for luck.

'Yeah, I remember. I read about it.'

'No one ever ask you about it?'

'Not until now.'

'You mind asking your colleagues if they know anything?'

The man nodded without saying anything.

'No one's under any suspicion. I'm just starting from scratch and trying to put the pieces together.'

The man nodded again, his suspicion and curiosity aroused.

He dropped me off at Borgo delle Colonne and asked for a small fortune. He stared at me closely as I handed over the cash. I realised that my face was bound to arouse interest for the next few days.

'Here, take this,' I said, slipping him a card. 'There's a reward for any information,' I lied.

I went into the bathroom and looked at myself in the mirror. I was shocked at what I saw. Only my cropped hair looked normal. My right eye had swollen mauve and my ear lobe was caked in dark red crusts. The lower lip of my mouth looked bloated. I tried to roll my shoulders, but each millimetre of movement hurt in different ways. I was surprised how the pain shot to my back or fingertips as I tried to move my arms. I swallowed some painkillers and crawled into bed. I fell asleep to the hypnotic sound of the rain lashing against the windows.

Thursday

Thursday morning. I had been getting dressed when the phone went. It was Mauro. I found the news more confusing than surprising.

'Salati', I heard him say, 'committed suicide.'

I thought it was him telling me his take on the Riccardo case. It sounded like a statement about what had happened to the young boy. But his voice was urgent and it was barely morning.

'What?' I said.

'Umberto Salati. He's committed suicide.'

'Are you sure?'

'I heard it from a friend.' Mauro told me the news. They had found Umberto outside his condominium early this morning. He had sky-dived from the top floor.

I kept hearing myself say I couldn't believe it.

'I heard this morning', Mauro said, 'when I was out buying the paper. Someone at the edicola told me.'

'Is it public yet? Is it on the news?'

'The radio said at six that a dead body had been found. They haven't formally identified it.'

'So how do you know it's him?'

'Because this guy seemed to know the details. He said Salati had jumped.'

'I can't believe it. You're sure it's Umberto Salati?'

'Like I say, it hasn't been confirmed. What are you going to do?'

'He lives in Via Pestalozzi, doesn't he?'

'By the cittadella.'

'I've got to go. Thanks Mauro.'

I threw the phone on the bed and finished getting dressed. It was freezing. I pulled on a jumper and went to put on the coffee.

Salati had committed suicide. Umberto Salati had jumped and I was the one who had pushed him to the edge. I had tried to break him and I had succeeded nicely. I don't normally feel guilt because I live, if I may say so, a pretty clean life. But now I felt guilt like an ice-cube in the heart. If it was true that Umberto was dead, I knew I was to blame.

It was still early and after last night's rain the sky was a slightly lighter grey than yesterday. I slugged the coffee and headed out towards the cittadella. The city was still asleep, just the odd bike or moped heading off to work.

As I got closer, though, there were people running towards Via Pestalozzi. It made me impatient to get there first and I started walking more quickly. There were carabinieri at either end of the street holding back people with microphones.

'Is it true?' I asked a man with a camera on his shoulder.

'Don't know.'

'What's the official line?'

'They've found a body.'

'Has someone tried to call him?' I didn't even need to mention Salati's name.

'No reply.'

I moved towards the carabinieri.

'What's happened?' I asked.

'There's been a suicide.'

'Have they identified the body?'

'No.'

The carabinieri didn't like privates muscling in, but I had to try. I showed them my licence but it didn't make any difference. I got the usual, dead-pan brush-off.

There was nothing to do. I went and sat in the bar at the corner of Via Solferino. Other journalists started turning up. Someone from *La Gazzetta*, one of the staff reporters from the local radio station, the local Rai guy.

Carabinieri kept coming and going. The first reliable confirmation we got was when one of the neighbours emerged from the condominium.

He was immediately besieged by the journalists and he seemed to enjoy the attention.

'Is it true it's Umberto Salati?' one of the journalists asked.

'It's unbelievable. Poor man. I had no idea he was, no idea he might . . .'

'Could you identify who it was?'

'Umberto,' he said, hearing the question for the first time. 'He was on his back, but his head was, it was horrible.'

I looked beyond the crowd. I had to get to the site, but it was still cordoned off. I had already shown my badge to the blank carabiniere this end of the street, so I did three sides of a rectangle, walking along Solferino to the Stradone, along that to Passo Buole so that I came at the street from the other end. An officer held up his hand as I approached.

'Forbidden,' he said.

'I live here.'

'What number?'

'Seventeen.' I pointed at a building and the carabiniere fell into step with me, expecting to accompany me to my door just to make sure. He kept looking back every few steps to check that no one else had ducked under the thin plastic ribbon.

I walked slowly knowing I would be allowed to pass only once. After they had realised I didn't live here, I would be hounded away with a choice insult. I slowed down even more as I came to the middle of the street. There was an ambulance, two carabinieri Alfa Romeos, and an unmarked car that was so badly parked it could only be the plainclothes.

Outside the block at number eight were men in white overalls taking measurements in the courtyard. I crouched down, pretending to be doing up my shoe-laces and saw between the various ankles a man's face.

The chin was unnaturally far from the shoulder. The yellowing moustache was red. I tilted my head and saw the contorted features of Umberto Salati: the thick hair, the round cheeks. It looked like he was asleep.

I had an involuntary intake of breath. Seeing it like that didn't leave much doubt about life and death.

I pretended that I had forgotten my keys and slinked away from my escort. I still couldn't believe it.

I tried to think straight. I had been in the game long

enough to know that something was suspicious. This had something to do with Riccardo. Whatever had started a couple days ago had caused Umberto Salati to jump. Or had persuaded someone to push him. Because it was always like this. A case was never just a case. It became many, each one knocking into the next. What I had assumed was a cold case had become suddenly hot. A bit of gentle sport had become dangerous.

I felt under threat myself, as if I were somehow responsible for what had happened. I was often tense on a case, but I never felt, like now, that I was somehow at the centre of it. It might even have been my aggressive openness the night before that had unhinged Salati.

I hated not being at the scene of the crime. If this really was a murder, every minute was precious. You needed to stop people moving. You couldn't let them into or out of the building. You had to do everything quickly: take statements, swabs, photographs, measurements, record number plates, request phone records, dust every handle and button in the building. I didn't trust the officials to be anything like thorough enough.

'What are you doing?' The voice made me jump and I stood up quickly. 'Castagnetti?' The voice sounded surprised.

It was Dall'Aglio. He had the same uniform as the young boy who had been escorting me, but he looked much older. 'You shouldn't be here. I'm going to have to move you on.'

'I'm sorry,' I said wearily.

'What are you doing here anyway? I know you're quick, but this isn't even public knowledge yet.'

'Tip-off.'

'Always a tip-off, eh?'

I looked at him, trying to work out if he was malleable. 'Was it really suicide?'

'I can't answer that, you know the rules.'

'What time did it happen?'

'There will be an official announcement later today.'

'What floor was he on?'

Dall'Aglio didn't say anything, but subtly put his index finger vertically upwards.

'Top?'

He nodded.

I looked at Dall'Aglio. We had been out for a drink together a couple of times but now he was in uniform and this was different. It was pointless to throw more questions his way.

'OK,' I said, 'OK. See you around.'

I walked a little further on and took out my binoculars. There was a row of trees shielding the building from the street. I moved further on to see the building better. It was a six-storey block. It looked elegant and large. Through the brass and glass doors you could see the dark banisters. The lighting was low. It looked typical for this chic part of town: large awnings overhanging balconies laden with leafy plants.

The top floor was surrounded by a terrace which formed a continuous balcony on all four sides. It had no plants. I could see an open door leading on to the balcony above where the body lay.

I moved my gaze downwards, past the trees to the gravel path where Salati had fallen. Closer towards me was a sloping concrete drive leading down to what was presumably the underground car park.

I put the binoculars back and ducked under the cordon the other side of the street. I pulled out my mobile and called Crespi.

'Umberto Salati is dead,' I said bluntly.

'Who is this?'

'Castagnetti. You hired me a few days ago, remember? Umberto Salati is dead. There's no official confirmation but I've been to the scene. It's him.'

For once he was speechless.

'We need to talk,' I said. I didn't want to go back to Crespi's office. The man seemed impregnable there. 'Let's meet in the square at eleven.'

I snapped the phone shut. I looked back one last time at the palazzo. There were armed guards at the front and back entrance. By the cordon I could see an old-fashioned Italian circus. I could see the carabinieri taking statements in the car park, and the reporters were then taking statements from the carabinieri. Both were then reporting those statements to their superiors who would publicise them when it suited.

The people coming out of the *cittadella* paused to look at the disorder and ask questions.

'What's going on?' people kept asking me. I shrugged so many times I got backache.

On the Stradone it was business as usual. Women in slack fur coats bustled along the pavements. They looked like hairy eggs. I saw a man carrying a dog in a Burberry handbag. A young girl was wearing a silver-grey Belstaff jacket, only it was imitation because the label said Belfast. Perhaps it was deliberate, a subversive logo. But it looked the same as the real thing. That was the important thing in this city: to look the part, to give off the signals if you only knew how.

I walked slowly towards the Circolo. I called Mauro and told him to meet me there. I wanted to do what the rest of the city would be doing: watch the story on TV.

Mauro was there before me, already nursing a glass of malvasia. The TV was on full volume. There were live feeds from Salati's house. Only hours after his death there were camera crews outside his palazzo, some conducting interviews with his neighbours via the intercom, others filming the roof terrace from below. Funny how police always let in their favourite journalists.

'What happened to you?' Mauro asked cheerfully. 'Looks like old Salati landed on you.'

On the TV, twenty police cadets were shown combing the gardens and shrubs below. Tall trees were being searched, prodded and pulled by policeman standing in the rectangular fist at the end of a crane's yellow arm.

Then there was an interview with the slippery mayor. He chose his words very carefully, as if he were trying to save himself from something: 'He was a dedicated man who represented the best of this city – enterprise, imagination, generosity. We are all in mourning. Our thoughts', the mayor was now looking into the camera, 'are with his family.'

As usual the institutional expressions of regret disguised any discord. I knew the official civility by now. It meant no one had a bad word to say against anyone who was dead. Death always made everyone wonderful.

'Are you personally convinced', the bald journalist asked the mayor, 'that Umberto Salati voluntarily took his own life?' It didn't look right and the little journalist obviously knew it. No one dared to ask such a question on live TV to such a powerful politician unless the piazza was with you.

The mayor drew breath slowly and nodded. 'From early indications it seems so. Although it does appear that Umberto Salati died by his own hand, I hope we remember him for the way he lived his life, not for the way in which he ended it.'

Mauro threw a shiny napkin at the set. 'Balle', he said. 'You know that "suicidarsi" isn't just a reflexive verb? Sometimes there's a subject and an object involved. It's something that someone does to someone else.'

'Yeah, I know,' I said. I had heard it all before: people were always being 'suicided'.

'You've got a crazy situation', said Mauro, 'where you might suspect Umberto of murdering Riccardo back in 1995, but at the same time you now suspect Riccardo of murdering Umberto over fourteen years later. And until you find Riccardo, walking or rotting, you won't know which one it is.'

'Maybe neither,' I said with resigned frustration. It was like trying to thread a needle with cooked spaghetti.

It was surely too much to think that Salati's death was Ricky's doing. Things like that just didn't happen. People didn't turn up out of the blue to commit a fatal push and disappear again. The only connection I could find between the brothers was some meaningless word like 'cursed' or 'jinxed'. Silvia Salati's sons were gone. And for the time being not even death connected them, at least not until I found Ricky's skeleton somewhere.

Even if Riccardo was alive, why would he bump off his brother? If it was greed, he surely would have done something before their mother died. That way her estate would all be his. As it was, Umberto's share of the estate would now pass to his ex-wife or their children. There didn't seem to be a motive.

Maybe it really was suicide. Maybe Umberto was distraught at the death of his mother, distraught at the fact that he might never have truly known who she was. He might have been filled with remorse for what had happened, or what he had done, to his brother. Maybe he thought I was closing in on him and had preferred to face death than face the music. There were certainly enough motives for suicide.

But it just didn't add up. Umberto didn't seem like a broken man. He seemed like the sort to get angry, to get even, rather than let life run him over.

Mauro switched to the other local channel. An anchorman announced an interview with Salati's grieving ex-wife from Traversetolo, Roberta. She was filmed stepping on to her doorstep to say she was saddened to hear of the death of her former husband, and that for the sake of their children the family would ask to be allowed to mourn in private.

'Auguri,' I said sarcastically.

I knew that the television would pollute everything about this case. It would be the source of all information. We always complain about the lack of justice in

Italy, about the fact that most iconic crimes in the country's history go unpunished. But that's largely because everyone expects clarity to come from the television. Its studio experts speculate on these *misteri*, they combine excited guesses with stoked indignation. Every new scoop pretends to offer clarity, but actually spreads confusion to keep the story going. That way the spectacle will never finish and it can be rewritten through barroom gossip. And then the *grande pubblico* will be able to show, through paranoia and fantasy, that you really can't believe in anything. In the end, everyone will have their own, breathtaking explanation for what happened in this or that tragedy.

I watched for another hour, hearing the same bulletins repeated every few minutes.

I wondered how much the carabinieri knew about Riccardo Salati, Umberto's missing brother. Dall'Aglio would be contacting me, that was for sure. I would almost be their first lead. That was something I didn't need: being leaned on by resentful uniforms who had nothing else to go on. The only advantage was that the information would have to go two ways. I would spill the little I knew about what had happened in 1995, and Dall'Aglio would let slip some forensic detail or anomalous alibi they had turned up.

I slugged the dregs of my wine and said goodbye to Mauro.

'Where are you going?' he asked, hurt.

I didn't say anything. I just slapped his shoulders and left the hardened drinkers of the Circolo to their favourite poisons.

I wandered aimlessly and listened to people's conversations. There's a saying that the city is so quiet that people whisper. That's what it seemed like this morning. There were small groups gathered together in the corner of bars, leaning close together so that no one else could hear. I could guess what they were saying. I had heard all the old men at the Circolo. I had heard people in the bus-stops. They were all asking about the Salati suicide and saying it sounded wrong. It was a mess which had been served up too neatly.

There was too much I didn't know. And even when I knew the facts, there might only be one pointer hidden amongst them all. Like the time Umberto Salati had returned home. Where had he been? Who he had spoken to? Who was in the block of flats? What had they heard?

My phone was ringing. I slid it open and before I even got it to my ear I heard a man's voice: 'Castagnetti?'

'Yes.'

'It's Mazzuli from *La Gazzetta*. We met the other day. We're running a story tomorrow about Umberto Salati's death.'

He hadn't said suicide and I felt on edge.

The journalist kept talking. 'Is it true you were investigating the disappearance of Riccardo, Umberto Salati's younger brother?'

I paused. I could hear the hack tapping his keyboard impatiently.

'What are you writing?'

'Just taking notes.'

'I haven't even said anything yet.' I couldn't be sure what he already knew. *La Gazzetta* was the official mouthpiece of the city's wealthy industrialists, and it didn't go out on a limb for a story like this without being very sure of its facts. If this man was being given space to write about the Salati death they must have had some information.

'I wanted to ask you a couple of questions. Is it true there's evidence Riccardo Salati is alive?'

So much for them knowing their facts. 'Absolutely none at all.'

'Didn't he publish a mourning notice in our newspaper on the occasion of his mother's death?'

'That was someone else,' I said disdainfully.

'Have you got any proof of that?'

'You know the answer to that.' I remembered the Visa slip that this same journalist had passed me only two days ago.

'You've traced the payment?'

'Sure,' I lied.

'Who made the payment?'

'I can't tell you that.'

'I thought we had a deal?'

'That doesn't include passing information to a journalist before it's passed to the appropriate authorities.' When I lie I become more self-righteous than an altar boy.

'Is it true Riccardo Salati is a suspect in his older brother's murder?'

I laughed. 'You're talking to the wrong man. I don't know who's a suspect any more than you or your chickens.'

'Do you believe the suicide story?'

Mazzuli was waiting for a reply. I didn't say anything and eventually I heard him fingertipping a keyboard.

'This is all off the record,' I said. 'You put my name in print and I'll never speak to you again. You with me?'

'Fair enough,' he said like he hadn't heard. 'So?'

'Put it this way: I would be amazed if it were suicide.'

'Let me ask you another question. Is it true Umberto was investigating Riccardo's death?'

'That's a more intelligent question.' I scratched a sideburn. It sounded loud inside my head.

'And?'

'He was probably doing something similar to yourself. Asking the wrong questions and getting the wrong answers.'

'Is that right?'

'Listen, you want a scoop on the Salati story, I'll give it to you the minute I find it, believe me. I'll call you. We had a deal and I'm a man of my word. But for now I know nothing about it other than what I've heard on TV.'

'Had you already interviewed Salati about his brother's disappearance?'

'No comment.'

'I'll take that as a yes.'

'You can take that as goodbye.' I hung up and stared at the phone. So much for trying to swap favours with a journalist. This was exactly what I had dreaded from the start. I was at the centre of a media storm.

Crespi was already waiting under the hooves of Garibaldi's horse when I arrived.

'You will obviously', the notary said first up, 'have to make a statement to the police about your own investigations.'

That angered me. Crespi was condescendingly telling me my own moral duty as if I didn't know what it was. I already knew that my poking around would have to be made public and I didn't need Crespi reminding me of it.

'My commission', I said slowly, 'was merely to verify the legal status of the subject Salati, Riccardo.'

'And had you already contacted the now deceased older brother?'

'Of course I had contacted him,' I spat. 'I interviewed him briefly in his shop, nothing more.'

My words sounded aggressive, and it shocked me how quickly I was brushing myself clean of a man who had only just died.

'Dear Castagnetti, they were brothers. You surely realise that their fates were in all probability linked? What happened to one is almost certainly related to what happened to the other.'

I didn't know what to say. It was undeniable. Crespi knew it. Riccardo might have been killed by Umberto, or – if you were imaginative – the other way round. Somewhere there was the crime of fratricide, that was likely. My problem was that if one of the brothers had murdered the other, that still left one dead body unaccounted for.

'What you tell the police is your business,' Crespi carried on. 'All I ask is that you provide me with a report regarding the legal status of my client's younger son, Riccardo.' He spoke as if he were dictating a letter.

'Coglione,' I said to myself as I walked away.

I walked back to my place in Borgo delle Colonne. I picked up the phone and dialled the number of the di Pietro woman in Rimini.

'You've heard then?' I said when she came to the phone.

'I heard.'

'Do you believe it?'

'What?'

'The suicide.'

'I don't know.'

'Where were you last night?'

She laughed. I repeated the sentence a little more slowly.

'I was here, with the family.'

'Giovanni and the children?'

'Right.'

'And they can confirm that can they?'

'Come and ask them. Where else would I be?'

I nodded to myself. It was far-fetched to see her wrestling Salati out of a window, but I had to ask. It was another fact that would need checking.

'You need to get a guard on Elisabetta,' I said.

'She's very safe here,' Anna said. 'What she needs is rest, not all this anxiety around her.'

'There's no point looking after her well-being if she's dead, you with me? Her uncle has been murdered, and her father has been missing for more than a dozen years. It wouldn't surprise me if she's next.'

The woman didn't say anything but was breathing heavily. I could hear little coughs like she was trying to get a fishbone out of her throat. It's strange listening to someone you don't know crying on the phone. Almost like listening to them have a shower through a bathroom door.

'I want to hire you,' she said.

'Why?'

'If she really is in danger, I need someone to look after her.'

'I'm already hired,' I said sadly. Working freelance is like waiting for a bus. Nothing turns up for ages, then everything comes at once.

'Couldn't you do both?'

'Conflict of interests, sweetness.'

'But you just said, she's in danger.'

'She might be. Call the police, let them know. Or call a private. There are enough in Rimini from what I remember. You could always call in the heavies from the Hotel Palace. Another thing, you're going to get a herd of hacks coming your way. They're probably on the Via Emilia as we speak.'

She didn't say anything. I didn't want to labour the point, but I had seen clients of mine in the past who had been in the blizzard of publicity and it was a cold and frightening place. It felt like the world was staring at you, sneering and pointing. 'Your number's in the book, isn't it? You might want to take the phone off the hook.'

*

By the time I got back to my office there was a small gathering of the city's worst journalists. I recognised Mazzuli there as well.

There was no point trying to blank them. We would have to come to some sort of deal.

They recognised me long before I even got to my front door. About half a dozen thrust microphones under my chin and asked me questions simultaneously so that I couldn't understand any of them.

'I'm only talking if that camera is switched off.'

The cameraman pointed it at the pavement and opened a grey plastic gate on the side of the machine to shut it down. All journalists were like predators, but the TV crowd were the worst.

'Right, I'm not making any comment until I've spoken to the relevant authorities.' There was a groan of disappointment from the journalists. 'I will happily talk to you as soon as I have arranged to share with my uniformed colleagues any information I might have regarding this case.'

They stared at me in silence, and then all started throwing questions. I walked inside and shut the door on them. I dropped the *tapparelle*, allowing the cord to run through my fingers just fast enough to warm them.

I sat down and dialled Dall'Aglio. As soon as I gave my name I was put through.

'Castagnetti,' said Dall'Aglio, 'just the man.'

'Did you give my name to the press?'

'Of course I didn't. If it's any consolation, we've probably got more journalists out here than Palazzo Chigi. There have been fifteen of them on my tail all morning.'

'Understandable. It is a murder.' I said it pointedly, trying to trip Dall'Aglio into an indiscretion.

'Listen, it's far too early to know what it is. My instinct says you're probably right, but I'm not going to go public until I'm very sure of the facts.'

'Which are?'

'You tell me.'

I didn't say anything.

'Had you spoken to Salati about your investigations?'

'Sure.'

'When?'

'Yesterday. In his shop. His assistant was there. I've been in regular contact with him ever since Monday.'

'No sign he had something like this in mind?'

'None at all. He was a man in mourning, he looked tired, but he wasn't broken. There's no way this was suicide. I feel, somehow, like I caused his death . . .' I let the sentence hang there, hoping Dall'Aglio would agree to cooperate.

'Meaning?'

'You'll reciprocate?'

'Don't I always? Go on, tell me . . .'

'It turns out Riccardo, the younger brother, wasn't quite what he seemed. He was the son of Massimo Tonin, the lawyer. Tonin had an affair with the Salati woman back in the 1970s. I told Salati as much yesterday and he was round there in a shot.'

'Where?'

'The Tonin estate.'

'You tailed him?'

'Sure.'

'And you saw him come back?'

'I saw him get back in his car, the black jeep, and leave the Tonin place. That was the last I saw of him until this morning.'

'What time did he leave their place?'

I looked at my notebook. 'Seven thirty-nine. If he went straight home, he would have been there by eight.'

Dall'Aglio was silent. It was probably the best lead they had and I thought I might as well pass on everything. 'There's something else. I've got a Visa slip for a payment that interests me.' I read the six numbers out of my notebook. 'Six Two Two Zero Four Nine. Put a trace on that and let me know.'

'What is it?'

'Someone appears to have been impersonating the younger brother. Published a notice of mourning in Monday's *Gazzetta*.'

'You're sure of this?'

I didn't reply because there wasn't any certainty about anything.

'You're sure it's not Riccardo himself?'

'I would be very surprised. But yeah, it's just about possible. Trace it.'

'OK. What else?'

'That's it so far.'

Dall'Aglio sighed.

'You?' I asked expectantly.

'Not much yet. The autopsy is due back this afternoon. That'll tell us more.'

'Who's doing it?'

'I don't know. One of the regulars. There's just one

thing that worries me at the moment. We haven't found his keys.'

'How do you mean?'

'We haven't got Umberto Salati's keys. It's a minor detail and I'm sure they'll turn up, but for the moment we haven't found any. Not on his person, and not in his flat.'

I frowned. That was something and Dall'Aglio knew it. He was pretending it was a minor irritant, but they would already have been through the flat with a tooth-comb and if they hadn't found the keys it meant they weren't there.

'The keys weren't on him?'

'Nothing in his pockets except cigarettes and a lighter.'

I suddenly had something to go on and felt restless. As always, it wasn't something so much as the absence of something. It didn't make sense that no keys had been found. It made the whole official narrative of the suicide seem implausible. If Salati had let himself into his flat, where were the keys? If they were in his pocket when he jumped, why weren't they on him when he was found? If Salati didn't have his keys, how had he let himself into the flat?

'It's definitely murder isn't it?'

Dall'Aglio gave a non-committal grunt. 'If so, we have another problem. There was no murder weapon.'

'Gravity,' I said. 'That and the ground.'

'And the push,' Dall'Aglio said, as if he was fantasising, imagining people behind Salati, pushing him off the balcony. 'I can imagine lots of people at his shoulders,

151

itching to give him a nudge. He had enough enemies from what I can work out.'

'Friends too,' I said, 'they're the real danger.'

'Bad friends are like beans,' Dall'Aglio said. 'They make noise behind your back.'

I laughed. 'He had more than noise behind him, by the look of it. You'll let me know about the autopsy and that Visa slip?'

'Yes, yes.'

I needed to get hold of Salati's shop assistant. I phoned a friend who had a small clothing boutique the other side of the piazza, on Via Nazario Sauro.

'It's Casta,' I said. 'You heard about Umberto Salati?'

'I heard just now. Is it one of your cases?'

'Not really. I'm investigating something else, but now this has come up. Listen, I wanted to know about Salati's assistant, Laura. You don't know her surname by any chance?'

'Laura? I know her. Cute chick.'

'A name?'

'Laura's all I ever heard her called.'

'Did they have something going on?'

'Umberto didn't employ girls unless something was going on, if you know what I mean. He liked a high staff turn-over, liked to keep everything fresh.'

'And you don't remember her name?'

'No idea. But I could ask the girl who works here on a Saturday, she would probably know. I'll call you back.'

The line went dead. I stared out of the window. There

were two men playing cards on the steps by the statue of Padre Pio.

The phone started ringing again. 'Laura Montanari, that's the name.'

I thanked him and reached for the phone book. There were hundreds of Montanaris. I could have found out which one it was from Dall'Aglio, but I wanted to work on my own. I phoned them one by one until a man came on the phone and started shouting about how the press should leave his daughter alone. That was a decent giveaway.

I wrote down the address and was there within a few minutes.

Her father answered the door.

'I've told you, she's not making any statement . . .' He stopped as he looked at my badge.

'Who are you?'

'Private investigator. I need to talk to your daughter. She knows me. I was a friend of Umberto Salati.'

Montanari looked at me with suspicion but opened the door. I walked inside and saw the young girl lying on a sofa. By the high standards of a shop assistant she was dressed down. It looked like she had been crying.

'I'm sorry,' I said quietly. Her father had left the room. 'When did you hear?'

'This morning. When he hadn't opened up I went round there.'

'To his?'

'Sure.'

'You reported it?'

She nodded. It looked like her eyes were going to overflow again, so I waited.

'You've got keys to his place?'

She looked up to see if her father was in earshot. 'Sure,' she said softly.

'I want to know about his keys. Were they all on one ring?'

'Big bunch, sure.'

'Could you describe Umberto's key-ring to me?'

'It was one of the free ones from the shop we give to our customers.'

'Have you got any here?'

'No. But I could show you . . .'

'What's written on them?'

'Just the name of the shop, Salati Fashions.'

'Did he ever forget them?'

'All the time.'

'How many times in the last month?'

'Three or four. He would normally call me just as I was going to bed. He would phone to ask me to let him into his flat. I was never sure whether he really had lost them, or whether it was a ruse to get me round there. That was part of the reason my father didn't like him. He would call me late at night, and I would have to go round there to let him in, and then usually I would go up and you know . . .' Tears fell off her cheeks on to her lap.

'You said your father didn't like him . . .'

'It's a turn of phrase. He wouldn't,' she looked at me incredulous. 'That's impossible.'

The thing about the keys still worried me. I knew

154

what I was looking for now, a key-ring with the Salati Fashions logo. I would have to find how many had been handed out as freebies to customers and suppliers. I figured that the fact that Salati was absent-minded meant those keys couldn't have given access to any secret part of Salati's empire. No reputation or fortune depended upon them. There would be no confession locked away in some safe. If Salati mislaid his keys all the time, it didn't seem likely that they led anywhere. Another dead end, I thought.

'And had he forgotten his keys last night?' I asked her. 'Did you let him in last night?'

She shook her head.

'What was he doing last night?'

'Nothing. He said he was going home to sleep. He had been shattered since his mother's illness. He hadn't stopped for months. He just needed to sleep. That's what he said.'

'Who else had keys to his flat?'

She shrugged.

'Did he have other women?'

She didn't say anything.

'Were there other women in his life?'

She looked up at me as if I had insulted her. 'There was his wife, his mother, if that's what you mean. They both had the keys to his flat.'

'How do you know?'

'Because they used to let themselves in to do his laundry, make his bed, that sort of stuff. Less so recently, but when I first got to know him they were always around.'

I shook my head. It always amazed me that grown men couldn't pull a sheet over a mattress.

It was a short drive to Traversetolo where Umberto's estranged wife Roberta lived. I found her place easily enough and rang the bell on the outside gate. There was no reply so I called the number.

'Pronto.'

'Signora, my name's Castagnetti. I'm a private investigator hired by your late mother-in-law to find her son, Riccardo. Could we talk? I'm outside.'

'Was it you who rang the bell just now?'

'Yeah.'

She didn't say anything. I looked at the condominium. It had long brass letterboxes at the entrance and it looked spacious and calm: there were a couple of armchairs by the porter's glass lodge with ashtrays on their arms.

'Ground floor,' she said.

The door clicked open and I walked in towards the main door. I stopped and looked at the block. It was the standard thing. They're all the same: six or so stories, a flat on each corner. I once saw an old painting of these kinds of places from way back. Then they had courtyards, communal areas on the inside. The flats were like lines of a square, and in the middle was a well with some chickens or some pigs. It had been beautiful, a perfect design for a sunny country.

But now, in these palazzi, the tiny communal part was on the outside: little patches of scrawny grass between the outer and inner gates, rickety bike racks and bins and curls of dog shit. That was it. You had no shared view. No one ever looked over the centre of the place, only at the fringes, at the cars speeding past.

She came out of a flat to the left as I was going through the inner door. She was a slim, blonde woman. She had a beautiful face with bright eyes. But there was a sadness about her. It looked like it had been with her long before Umberto died.

'I'm sorry about your husband,' I said as she showed me in.

'He was an ex,' she said, bowing her head slightly as if to acknowledge the condolences. 'You knew him?'

'I met him on Monday, as soon as I was hired. When did you last speak to him?'

'At the funeral on Tuesday.'

'And you had a cordial relationship?'

'Friendly enough. We had fewer arguments after separation than we did before, that's for sure.'

'Why did you separate?'

'I don't think that matters now, do you?'

There was something mechanical about her, as if she was getting by out of habit. I had seen it before, the pride and defiance of a middle-aged woman bringing up children on her own. It was as if she were proving a point all the time, trying to show that she could still be attractive, but in doing so only showed that she had mislaid her spontaneity.

'He was a good man and a good father,' she said. 'He just couldn't stick to one woman. But he was always generous and warm. That's what all those girls saw in him, I suppose. He lavished presents on them, the same as he had with me when we met.'

I looked at her. It sounded like a wife trying to show her late husband's best side, trying to justify his behaviour.

'He told me that the night his brother went missing, in June 1995, he was with you.' I looked at her. 'Can you confirm that?'

'To be completely honest, I have no memory of where I was that night, but I remember telling police years ago that we were together that evening, and if I said that then, it must have been that way.'

'But you don't remember?'

'Do you remember where you were on a given night fourteen years ago?'

I shrugged. 'I probably would if it was the night my brother-in-law was murdered.'

She looked at me with disdain.

'Was there any rancour between the two of them, between Ricky and Umberto?'

'They didn't exactly get on. They were competitive.'

'And what happened between them the year Ricky went missing? In 1995?'

She drew a deep breath.

'I knew that Umberto had lent him a lot of money. I knew because it meant we couldn't move house that year. Umberto had found out that he was borrowing money from all and sundry and they had quite an argument.' She looked at me as if she didn't want me to get the wrong impression. 'But he was incapable of . . . there's no way he would have ever . . .'

'Did his disappearance have an effect on Umberto?'

'To be honest, he didn't seem unduly worried at the time. It had happened before. And then, when it became clear Ricky wasn't coming back, I think Umberto was more concerned about the effect on his mother.'

'And recently?'

'I think he changed when he saw Silvia dying. I think he longed to be able to bring news of Ricky to her dying bedside, even if it was only confirmation of what they all feared.'

'What made you think that?'

'I inferred it from the way he was speaking to the boys recently.'

'Your children?'

'Sure. He was always talking to them about the importance of the family, of looking after your own, of loyalty.'

'Did he think Ricky was still alive?'

She paused. 'I don't think so. I think he knew he was never going to find him. But he was looking for him, trying to work out what had happened.'

'You're sure about that?'

'What?'

'That he was investigating Ricky's disappearance?'

'Sure. He told me about it at the funeral.'

'On Tuesday?'

She nodded. 'We were standing beside each other at the burial and he whispered to me about his desire to sort everything out once and for all. Umberto liked the idea of playing the hero. He felt like he had to avenge those who had insulted his family. He got very worked up when talking about it.'

I listened to her as she spoke. She talked with precision and speed and I imagined she was a strict mother.

'Have you thought,' I said slowly, 'that the reason Umberto was keen to find Ricky was merely this: he wanted his mother's money and wanted to confirm his brother's death. He didn't want to share the jackpot with anyone else.'

She looked at me closely with her eyes almost shut. 'I thought exactly the same thing. I can't pretend I didn't.'

'And now that Umberto's dead, it makes a big difference to your family.'

'Finding Ricky?' She laughed, amused at the optimism.

'But it does, doesn't it?'

She stopped laughing and looked at me seriously.

'It makes a difference financially doesn't it?' I said again. 'Your mother-in-law died and left an estate. Now your husband is dead and your boys might be millionaires.'

'Sure. Sure it does. It makes a difference to my boys.'

'If Ricky can be proved to have died prior to Silvia Salati,' I wanted to make sure she knew the situation, 'then Umberto inherits the whole of his mother's estate. And now he's dead, your children might be very wealthy. If it was the other way round, half of what Umberto was expecting goes up in smoke.' I paused.

'Of course it does, I've just said it does. Is there anything else you want?'

Her warmth had gone and she was preparing to usher me out.

'Do you think the two are linked?' I said, standing my ground.

She was shaking her head nervously, like a horse being badly handled. It was as if she didn't want to think about the implications.

'And last night,' I said, 'where were you?'

'I was here, with the children.'

'Are they in?'

She put a hand on my chest. 'Keep them out of this. They're mourning their father.'

I left her there and apologised for the disturbance.

Friday

I was sitting in the bar opposite the carabinieri barracks watching my hands move from force of habit. My thumb and forefinger took the corner of a sugar sachet and shook it before ripping it open and emptying the contents into the piping black coffee. My right hand took up the spoon and stirred it.

Every morning millions of us perform exactly the same gestures learnt from observation. Having a coffee is as ritualistic as taking communion and I couldn't do it any differently to anyone else.

I stretched over to a next-door table and picked up the morning's edition of *La Gazzetta*. Even the news was ritualistic. The way the whole Salati case was reported followed a tried and trusted path: the reporter used the same phrases that are used every time a murder is committed. This was the 'Salati Giallo'. They never missed a chance to churn out the old *giallo* label. That word – meaning both 'yellow' and 'thriller' – makes dark crimes sunlit and exciting. In this charming country, even death is made sumptuous.

I read the rest of the paper. There were the usual stories: left-wing extremists scribbling threatening graffiti under the houses of union leaders and politicians; something about the motor show preparations; an article about the discovery of archaeological remains in the suburbs which would slow up the work on the metro; a visiting academic from Spain was compared to half a dozen people I had never heard of.

This is where all the carabinieri came for refreshment throughout the day. Dall'Aglio was late for our appointment and was immediately dismissive of my insistence on locating Salati's keys.

'Even supposing what you say is true,' he whispered in the crowded bar, 'why would a person keep the keys? If Salati was pushed, gravity was the only killer. If you haven't got a murder weapon, the keys are as close as you'll get. It's like having a hot gun in your pocket. No one would have kept hold of them.'

'Unless the murderer was under the impression that Salati's keys were of importance, that they might lead to evidence which was even more incriminating.'

'Like what?' Dall'Aglio said impatiently.

'Maybe Salati was investigating his younger half-brother's disappearance when he was murdered. The murderer might have kept the keys in the hope of destroying any discoveries which Salati had committed to paper.'

'It sounds very far-fetched to me.'

'Everything's far-fetched until it becomes fact,' I said quickly. I knew I was clutching at straws, but Dall'Aglio didn't seem concerned to clutch at anything. 'There are other possibilities,' I went on. 'They took the keys, for whatever reason, and then realised what you have just said: that they were a smoking gun. So they ditched them.'

'You want my men to find a bunch of keys which could be anywhere between here and Potenza. How do you expect us to do that?'

I shrugged. 'I don't know. But until they turn up, you won't get a conviction in this case.'

'I don't mean to be disparaging, Castagnetti,' Dall'Aglio said, 'it's just that I don't see what, practically, I can do to test your theories. We're talking about a case in which not only do we not have any leads to the murderer, we honestly don't even know if there was a murder at all.'

I was impatient. When something needs doing, I like to get it done. I don't mind Dall'Aglio, he's a hard-working, honest official, not something there's exactly a surplus of. But he's a stubborn, officious official. He has to justify every action to his superiors and that makes him more cautious than a blind dog crossing the motor-way.

'When was the autopsy?' I changed tack.

'They did it yesterday.'

'Who?'

'Garrone I expect. I'll check.'

I stood up and bowed sarcastically.

I would have to approach it from the other side. Slip something to the press to put pressure on him, or else hire some staff myself. I could have done with two dozen men to command like Dall'Aglio had. He could comb a field quicker than he could comb his hair.

I walked down the street and asked myself why I bothered. I always say it's the money, but if that was the case, I would hire staff and we could film every infidelity this side of Reggio. That's a racket if ever there was one. But like I said, I don't do infidelity. It's no different to blackmail in the end and you end up selling your pics to the highest bidder.

So it's more than just the money. I go through all this dirt because I'm fed up with everyone settling for appearances, fed up with conceitedness and *menefreghismo*. I've had it with the good life, the luxuries and the reputations that no one wants to offend. I don't think my line of work is anything special. It's usually grubby and aggressive. It's fraught and frustrating. But it's honest. It's a bit like gardening: you're never quite sure what's going to come up, you work hard and keep guessing, just trying to keep things alive. And once in a while you can sit back and think you might have made a tiny corner of the world a better place.

I walked towards the Ponte di Mezzo. The river was a furious torrent now. All the snow in the mountains was melting and the river was surging through the city. The water curled and crashed only a few centimetres below the arches of the bridges, speeding away towards the Po with its cargo of tree trunks and drowned animals. The noise was so loud that you could barely hear anything else. The water was pounding under the bridge, speeding past but keeping exactly the same shape, the same frenetic rolls and whirlpools.

I walked to the other side of the bridge and only there did the roar of the water subside. That sudden change in volume shifted something in my brain. Maybe it was the image of that water, that sense that the real action of a bridge is not above it but below. All that water and talk about the keys had set something off. What happened to Salati, I realised, hadn't happened upstairs, in the building, up top. It must have happened below.

I pulled out my phone and tried to get through to the pathology department. A sleepy voice came to the phone.

'Garrone?'

'Sì.'

'My name's Castagnetti. I'm working on a case and I believe you did the autopsy.'

'I know you. You're that private dick.'

I made a grunt. 'You did an autopsy . . .'

'I do dozens every day.'

'Must be fun. The man's name was Salati.'

'The guy who used to have a shop on Via Cavour?'

'Exactly.'

'I zipped him up yesterday.'

'And?'

'The tidiest suicide I've ever seen.'

'What do you mean?'

'He was over ninety kilos, but his fall was so light he didn't break a bone in his body.'

'He didn't jump?'

'If he did, he flew down.'

'So why's everyone talking about suicide?'

'Guesswork.'

'So what killed him?'

'Head injuries, sure, but not from falling to the ground. I would say it was something with a series of small, sharp protrusions . . . like an athlete's spikes, or football boots with sharpened studs.'

'You're sure about this?'

'There's not much certainty about death but some things seem quite probable.'

'Like it's long.'

'Yeah, right.' The man laughed. 'His skull and neck and back were perforated with these little indentations.'

'How big?'

'Fairly tiny. There were between eight and fifteen spikes for each blow. On the skin you can just see the outline of the shape holding those spikes. It's slightly larger than a postage stamp. It wasn't the spikes that killed him – they're fairly shallow – it was the force behind them. It was some kind of hammer . . .'

'You've got photographs of these wounds?'

'Sure. Sent them up to Dall'Aglio yesterday.'

'Time of death?'

'We got the body yesterday morning. He had been dead roughly twelve hours. That puts the time between nine and eleven the evening before.'

I put the phone down. If Salati hadn't fallen from his balcony, it meant that a woman could have been responsible. There might not have been a fight up there at all. It might have happened on the ground and he might have been hit from behind. Someone had tried to make it look like suicide, gone upstairs to open a window, tried to make it look like a jump. It was an amateur, that was for sure.

It wasn't surprising that Dall'Aglio wasn't publicising the news. He had enough media interest around him without them getting even more excitable. But it would come out sooner or later. The *giallo* would become a murder. It would go national by tonight.

My phone was vibrating.

'Sì.'

'Castagnetti?' It was Dall'Aglio.

'Why didn't you tell me it wasn't a jump? Salati died on the ground.'

'You've spoken to Garrone?'

'Sure. So much for swapping favours.'

'I've told you before, I don't trade favours. But I've got something for you. You're going to like this. My women in the finance department have traced the Visa record for the *Gazzetta* payment.'

'Go on.'

'Unfortunately it's not Riccardo. I half hoped we would hear that it was genuine, that it really was your boy. As it is, I really don't understand it.'

'Give me the name,' I said impatiently.

'Massimo Tonin, the lawyer.'

'Tonin?' I laughed.

'What's so funny?'

'It's not funny, so much as . . .' I shook my head. Humans never cease to surprise me, but Tonin was certainly a weird one. 'I got the impression he really cared for that boy.'

'Maybe that's why he paid to put a piece in the paper.'

'You don't believe that?'

'I don't know what to believe any more.'

'I reached that point a long time ago.' I couldn't understand why old Tonin would want to pretend to be Riccardo in print. Unless he didn't want people to think he was dead, unless he wanted people to think his boy was alive and well.

'We're going to bring him in,' Dall'Aglio said.

I felt my limbs tense up. Once he was in custody he would be all buttoned up. I would have no element of surprise. I wanted to race round to his now, before they brought him in.

But I couldn't do that. I couldn't race round there on information Dall'Aglio had just given me. Dall'Aglio would accuse me of interference and *favoreggiamento*. I would have to come in on Dall'Aglio's coat-tails.

'I'll come,' I said.

Dall'Aglio didn't say anything.

'As an observer. Nothing else.'

Dall'Aglio was still silent. He must know, I thought, that this was my case as well as his. It was my information that gave him the breakthrough.

'All right,' said Dall'Aglio. 'You know the rules. You don't touch anything, you don't say anything.'

'Right. When's the arrest?'

'We're going there now. Wait for us on Via Trento by the cinema.'

I put the phone down and went out. Tonin was a strange one. He had seemed to me one of those astute lawyers. He might sell his soul for a few percentage points, but I couldn't see him knocking off his own son. But then, you never think that when you first set eyes on someone. There is no dark streak, not until you know someone's killed another human being and you put that streak on them yourself. They're just ordinary people who do something irreversible. They're all different, and Tonin might be just one more specimen for me to study.

Dall'Aglio picked me up in the force's luxury Alfa Romeo.

'You armed?' Dall'Aglio asked as soon as I opened the car door.

'Sure.'

'Give it to me.'

I reached inside my jacket and passed him the pistol. It wasn't because Dall'Aglio didn't trust me. He knew me well enough not to worry about me getting twitchy if it got tense. It was a power thing. It meant he was in complete control of the operation. I admired the formality, even though I didn't like going after a suspect with only my bare fists.

Tonin came to the door before Dall'Aglio had even rung the bell. He stood there like a condemned man as Dall'Aglio read him his rights. Two officers then bundled him into the car. That was it.

'I'm taking him to the station. You coming?' Dall'Aglio said.

'I'll have a look round.' I replied. There was no point going back to the station. We would hang around for at least two or three hours whilst they searched for evidence to lay on Tonin's plate. I calculated that I might as well hang around and watch what happened at the house.

I went inside. The cadets were surprisingly efficient. Everything was turned upside down very neatly. I had expected them to send in the heavies, but it was all very deferential.

They went through all the drawers, pulled them out and looked underneath and behind. They took pictures off the walls, leafed through the books and magazines. The bathroom was pulled apart. They lifted up the shower tray and dismantled the bath. They listened to the plumbing and examined the surface of the soil in the garden. They went through the cypress and poplar trees with sticks. Still looking for those keys, I thought.

I wandered upstairs. It was a house like you used to see in American movies: a staircase wide enough for large plants where it turned a corner. The corridor upstairs was long and all lit up. Beings covered in white overalls kept coming out of rooms to the left and right.

I pushed into a room that looked like an old man's place. There were suits in the wardrobe, a single tooth-brush and razor in the bathroom. I took the top off a rectangular bottle of aftershave and sniffed it. It smelt like Tonin.

The couple obviously slept apart because the next room along was feminine. The wardrobe was full of designer outfits in garish colours. On the reproduction chest of drawers were photographs of the same man. He was good-looking in an overdone sort of way. He had long curling hair and facial hair which changed in each photo: a goatee in one, long, narrow sideburns in another. He must have spent half an hour shaving every day. There was a large photo where the man was wearing yellow corduroys. His brogues looked like the narrow nib of a fountain pen and they had fat, external stitching as if to pretend they were done by hand instead of by a machine. It looked like the same guy from the photo in Tonin's office.

'Who's that?' I asked one of the cadets taking tape samples from the carpet.

'No idea.'

I looked at the photographs again. I assumed it was their son Sandro because he was everywhere. There wasn't anyone else, no sibling to rival his place on his mother's chest of drawers. He must have thought he was an only child until poor Riccardo came along.

I went back downstairs and saw the huge hall. It was cold and unloved. Even the sofa against the far wall looked austere, like it had never been sat in. The cushions were placed at deliberate angles. I remembered when I had come in here two days ago how the woman's voice had bounced off the walls. I closed my eyes and tried to recall that atmosphere when we had first walked in. She had been on the phone.

I got to the bottom of the stairs and saw the handset. She had been speaking to someone. I got out my mobile and called Dall'Aglio. He was still in the car by the sound of it.

'I've got something else for you. Find out who their phone operator is and get an itemised breakdown of the calls from the Tonin house on Wednesday night.'

Dall'Aglio said nothing. He wasn't happy taking dictation from a rival.

'Has Tonin said anything?' I asked.

'Nothing. Says he will reply to questions in the presence of his lawyer.'

I laughed and hung up. Why a lawyer needed another lawyer to defend himself I couldn't understand. It made it look like the truth wasn't enough for him. He wanted to find a way out, and that meant calling in a colleague to help.

I went outside on to the drive and walked slowly towards the gate. I dialled the switchboard sweetheart.

'Studio Tonin.'

'That Serena?'

'Sì.'

'Castagnetti here.'

She didn't say anything.

'How you doing?' I asked.

'Fine. Can I help you?' She sounded distant, as if there were someone listening to her talking.

'Sure you can. In the next hour or two a call is going to come in from jail. It will be Massimo Tonin, asking to speak to one of his colleagues.'

'Massimo's been arrested?' She sounded indignant.

'He has.'

'What for?'

'I don't know. Here's what I need you to do. As soon as you've put the call through, phone me and let me know who he asked to speak to.'

'I can't do that.' You would have thought I had asked her to show me her thighs.

'It's very simple,' I repeated. 'I'll give you my number.' I started giving her the numbers and she didn't interrupt.

'You got that? And you call me. Just one name. It's for Massimo's benefit. Take my word.'

'I don't know what your word's worth. I don't know you.'

'I know a really good way to get to know someone,' I said.

'I'm sure you do.'

'Call me.' I hung up before she could protest.

I had wandered back into the house and into the kitchen as we had been speaking. It was a large room with a central island of speckled granite. Above it hung huge pans and ladles. In one recess to the right was a large cooker where a pan was bubbling away.

Teresa Tonin came in from a far corner just as I was about to go out. She had an apron on which was smeared with flour. She suddenly saw me and jumped slightly with the surprise.

'You,' she said.

'You heard your husband's been arrested?'

'Of course I have. I've had men crawling all over my house for the last hour.' She looked at me bitterly, her lips pursed in anger. 'It's not enough that he publicly humiliated me by having that boy. To think that he could have done something even worse, so much worse. Not just give life to him, but . . .'

'But what?'

She didn't say anything.

'What did Umberto Salati want with you two days ago?' I asked.

She sighed heavily and then seemed to snap out of her reverie. 'Sorry?'

'Was Umberto Salati after money? The first words you said to me were over the intercom. "You're not getting anything from us," you said, or something similar.'

She stared at me. 'He was after money, sure.'

'Why?'

'He was threatening to tell the authorities about Massimo.'

'What about Massimo?'

'About Massimo's affair with that Salati woman.'

'Why would you pay him not to talk?'

'I wouldn't. That's what you heard me say, wasn't it? Everyone seems to know about it now anyway. I've no idea why that Umberto Salati thought he could get money from us. The innocent can't be blackmailed, isn't that right?'

'So why did Umberto think he could get money out of you? Because Riccardo had in the past?'

She had been about to turn her back and slice an onion, but she turned to face me.

'Was Riccardo blackmailing your husband back in '95?'

She held my stare and the earth seemed to stop turning for an instant. She didn't say anything.

'Tell me again,' I said slowly, 'what Umberto Salati wanted on Wednesday when he came round here.'

She looked at me with fiery, impatient eyes. 'He said Massimo was a disgrace. Said he had humiliated his mother. He said he knew everything, said he would hand it all over to the authorities.'

'What did he mean by that?'

'I don't know. I didn't understand it.'

178

It clearly meant something to her. 'What did you think he meant?'

'I assumed . . . I don't know. He said Massimo would pay for it. Said he could pay now or later, but he would pay.'

'Did he mention figures?'

'All he said is that he wanted the proof his brother was dead.'

'And he thought he could find it here?' She looked at me with anger, so I asked her another. 'So who did you phone?'

She froze. 'I phoned . . .'

'And then Salati was murdered?'

She stared at me with fury now. 'What exactly are you accusing me of?'

'Who did you phone?' I pressed.

She started walking towards me with a finger taking aim at my face. 'Get off my property. Get out of here.'

'Want me to call the police?' I said, and turned away.

'Castagnetti?'

'Serena?'

'The name's Giulio Tanzi.'

'Thank you. Put me through.'

The phone rang once and he picked it up.

'You the counsel for Tonin?'

'I don't talk to the press,' he said straight off.

'I'm not the press. Not police either. My name's Castagnetti.'

'And?'

'I'm a private.' The lawyer hesitated so I tried to say it quick, before he could interrupt. 'Your colleague Massimo Tonin has been arrested and the charge is pretty serious. Wouldn't look good for your firm to have a murderer in the ranks. Clients could kind of back off if they heard that. But I've got some great news for you. This charge won't stand up any more than a new-born baby.'

'How so?'

I brought him up to speed on the case. Told him what he already knew, like old Tonin was a gent, and some stuff he didn't, like the *Gazzetta* payment in Riccardo's name which was paid for with Tonin's card.

'What do you want?' he asked when I had finished.

'I want to interview him.'

'What's your interest?'

'Professional satisfaction. Proving someone wrong. The usual reasons.'

'If you do interview him, I will expect to be present.'

'Fine. I'm sure your presence would help.' I caressed the man's vanity. 'The whole city will be knocking on your door by tonight, pleading for an interview. You're in the spotlight like you've never been before. You're defending the most famous accused in Emilia-Romagna and you're about to clear his name.'

'Let me talk to my client and I'll call you back.'

He phoned as I was driving to my office. Tonin had agreed to see me immediately.

I walked over there and went down into the pit where he was being held with seven other men. He looked like a caged animal, pacing his confined space with frustration. He was still dressed in suit and tie.

The guards let him out and escorted us into an interview room.

'What does he want?' Tonin said to his lawyer as he looked at me.

'He wants to ask you some questions. He wants to help you.'

He stared at me. 'How are you going to help?'

'By proving you had nothing to do with Umberto's murder.'

He shook his head. He was contradicting me, as if he wanted to be charged in person, like he actually wanted to be accused of it.

'Why did you place a mourning notice in *La Gazzetta* under the name of a missing man?'

He stared at me but didn't deny it. It almost seemed to surprise him.

'Why', I fixed him, 'would you do a thing like that?'

He sighed. 'I don't know. Why would someone do that?'

'It's a very unusual thing to do if you haven't got a motive.'

'Maybe I felt sorry for her.'

'For Silvia Salati?'

'Sure. I thought the idea of her dying not knowing about our son was too much. I wanted to think that somewhere out there he actually was mourning her.'

'Who says he isn't?'

He looked angrily at me. 'What do you really want?'

'Try the truth. Why did you pay to publish a mourning notice under the name of a missing person?'

'I told you. I liked the idea of a son mourning his mother.'

'That sounds phoney to me.'

'That's how it was. It was harmless.'

'Harmless acts have a habit of turning nasty.'

We looked at each other like cats about to fight. But I had lost the element of surprise. Old Tonin had improvised his story and was sticking to it. He had paid, he said, for a mourning notice out of compassion. It was bull, but I had nothing to disprove it. I decided to change tack.

'Where was your wife on Wednesday night?'

'At home,' he said, 'you saw her yourself.'

'I saw her at seven-thirty,' I corrected. 'Umberto Salati died a couple of hours later. More than enough time for her to get into town. You've got separate bedrooms,' I said quickly. 'She could quite easily get up and go out without you noticing it.'

'Sure. Where's she going to go? She doesn't drive.'

That was a turn-up. It was either a last-minute lie, the sort of no-hoper people throw out when the game is up. Or it was true and I was barking up the wrong tree.

'She doesn't drive?' I tried not to make it sound like a question, as if I had known as much all along.

'Never has. If you think she walked into the city you're out of your mind. My wife doesn't walk anywhere.'

'Bicycle?'

'Sure. On the tangenziale in that fog. Not even you believe that, Castagnetti.'

I had been thrown off balance. I couldn't understand why a man who kept protesting his innocence still wouldn't explain what he was up to. I had yet to hear a rational explanation for that mourning notice. Maybe Tonin wasn't as rational as he appeared. Perhaps he had published the mourning notice because he wanted to see it, he longed to believe it. People will believe anything if they want it to be true, even little lies they've sown themselves.

'So why did you pay for a mourning notice in the name of Riccardo Salati? I've yet to hear a rational explanation.'

Tonin was shaking his head. He couldn't say anything, but I knew he was protecting someone. And it wasn't his wife. It didn't sound to me like he was particularly inclined to protect her at all. But he was protecting someone else.

'How many kids you got, other than Riccardo?'

'Just Sandro.'

'He's the one with long hair?'

Tonin nodded. He had his head in his hands, his palms almost covering his ears as if he didn't want to hear any more.

'Why don't you tell me about Sandro?' I said gently.

Tonin looked up at me and shrugged. It wasn't convincing but he wasn't going to say anything. I wasn't sure the old man even knew himself what his son had been up to. Or perhaps he had only just realised.

I tried another angle. 'This money you say you were giving the boy, who knew you were giving it to him?'

Tonin frowned, uncertain where the question was coming from.

'Did your family know you were giving the boy money?'

'Not that I know of, no.'

'You kept it secret?'

'Not particularly.'

'So someone could have found out about it?'

'Very easily. Everyone knows where my filing cabinet is, all my accounts are kept there.'

I looked at the old man. He seemed sincere, almost dignified in his despair. There was something about his glazed look that made me think he really had only just worked out what was going on.

'Which telephone company do you use?' I asked.

The man frowned.

'Which operator do you use at home?'

'Infostrada,' he said quickly, as if angry at the irrelevance of the question.

'You're still not telling me everything, Tonin.' I stood up. 'There will come a time when the murderer of your son Ricky is going to stand trial for this, and it would be just as well for you if it don't look like you had aided and abetted.' I picked a pen out of my jacket pocket and passed it to him. 'Write down what you know. It will help.'

Even the force of looking up at me seemed too much for him, but he took the pen out of my hand and nodded. He looked almost grateful that the time had come.

*

I went back to see Dall'Aglio but was kept waiting over an hour. Once I was admitted it was made clear that my presence was a distraction. He was reading report after report, calling people into his office to pick up a folder or bring in another. He was aloof and I didn't like it.

I tried to needle him by telling him about Tonin. 'Tonin's not involved, at least not how you think.'

'Criminals sometimes seem invincible,' Dall'Aglio said, 'and you feel therefore impotent. That is why so many of us take these crimes personally. They are an affront to our professional powers.' He looked at me as if he expected applause for his insight.

I shrugged.

'Did you get a trace on the phone call from the house that evening? Their phone company is Infostrada.'

'I know. I've got the list of calls in front of me.' He said it slowly, enjoying watching my impatience. 'There appears to have been only one phone call from the Tonin house that evening.'

'Go on.'

'0521–498444.'

'And who is it?'

'We haven't checked.'

'Thanks'.

Dall'Aglio looked up, wondering whether the gratitude was sarcastic. 'Now you. Why are you so interested?'

I decided I couldn't drop half a brick. I might as well drop the lot. 'Tonin lent the boy some money. The boy disappeared.'

'And you think Tonin . . .'

'No. I think the person who answers,' I looked down at his notebook, '0521 . . .'

'Did what exactly?'

'I don't know. But the way I see it, the only person pissed off when Ricky started paying off his debts was someone on Tonin's side of the fence. When Tonin started opening his purse to his bastard son, the only person who really cared was his son Sandro.' I looked up at Dall'Aglio to see if he was following me. 'Pass me the phone.'

Dall'Aglio obeyed as if it had been a command from a superior. I smiled with as much falsity as I could muster. Before letting go of the handset, Dall'Aglio put it on loudspeaker.

I punched in the numbers as I read them. There was a long pause and then the line began its long beeps.

'Sì?'

'Is that Sandro Tonin?'

'Speaking.'

I hung up and smiled smugly now. I looked at Dall'Aglio who was nodding and frowning at the same time.

'She phoned her son,' he said. 'That's all. It's a mother calling her son, nothing else.'

'It's him, trust me. Teresa Tonin phoned her son to say that Umberto Salati had been round. She told him Salati knew everything. He knows about the boy, she must have said, he knows about the bastard.'

I got up.

'Where are you going?'

'I'm going to have a chat with Sandro.'

*

186

It wasn't hard to find where the city's only Alessandro Tonin lived. I watched the flat for over an hour before a man came out.

I recognised him from the photographs. Facial hair in thin lines, long hair, expensive clothes.

I followed him to a hairdresser's salon, one of the spacious, expensive salons in the city centre.

I watched from outside and saw him hand over his coat and bag to a girl. He sat himself down to read a magazine.

I looked up at the 1950s board above the shop. I called Pagine Gialle and asked for the number of the place. They gave me the number immediately. I dialled it and saw a girl pick up the phone. She had a short white coat and coffee-coloured tights.

'Can I help?'

'I'm an investigator,' I said. 'I'm standing outside your salon. The man who just walked in, the guy with long curls, he's under investigation. He just handed you his bag and jacket. I'm going to walk into your salon in thirty seconds. I'm going to show you my badge and you're going to take me to the cloakroom. You understand?'

'You sure do talk quick,' she said in a whisper.

'What's your name?'

'Sveva.'

'Sveva? OK,' I hung up and walked between cars.

She smiled at me as I walked in.

'Hello stranger,' she said as if she were greeting an old friend. I looked at her legs as she led me to the back of the salon.

187

'In here,' she said as we went through two doors. She led me into a small cloakroom. We were pushed close together by the shoulders of the clients' thick coats. 'First show me your badge,' she said.

I pulled out my licence.

'But you're private.'

'Same thing. Still trying to keep scum off the streets.'

She looked at me with a come-on smile. 'You've got me into a cupboard under false pretences. You don't even look like an investigator.'

'You wanted a trilby and a magnifying glass?'

'No, it's just you look so normal.'

'Thanks,' I said, not sure it was a compliment. At least it was an improvement on comments about my swollen face. 'Show me his bag.'

'What's he done?' She passed me a leather shoulder bag and ripped off a sticker.

I pulled out his diary and spun the pages. I looked at dates and appointments but nothing stood out. A set of keys were in there.

'How long's he in for?' I asked the girl.

'He's having highlights. Could be an hour.'

'Highlights?' I shook my head. The guy was one of the peacocks. 'Is there a back way out?'

She nodded and opened the door to the cloakroom. 'Out there.'

I put the keys in my pocket and walked out the back. There was a dirty white door that looked out on to a courtyard car park. I followed the driveway back to the main road and went to the key cutters in Via Sauro.

'I need the whole bunch done. I've got fifty for you if you can do it in ten minutes.'

The man looked up at me like he wasn't used to being rushed. But he took the keys and fixed the first one into his vice. He pressed a button and the large metal box began to whine. Metallic dust flew off. Once the new key was done, the man went back over it, his hand rising and falling with the contours of the key's canines. He put the key by the counter and started with the next one.

Once he had done all eight he lined them up on the counter. I picked them up and compared them to the originals. The only difference was that the old were cold, the new warm. I blew a bit of dust off them.

'That'll be fifty euros,' the man said, proud of his profession.

'Thank you.' I put the note on the counter.

I retraced my steps and let myself in the back door to the salon. I went into the cloakroom where a girl I hadn't seen before was hanging a coat. She looked shocked to see me.

'Sveva around?' I asked.

She relaxed and said she was out front. I dropped the keys back into Sandro's bag and walked out the front way. The smell changed as I opened the door back into the salon. It smelt of expensive soap. The music was on loud, though you could only just hear it above the drone of driers.

Sandro had rectangles of aluminium foil in his hair. He was reading a magazine. Even in this bright light his tan looked dark and perfect. He had cold, blue eyes.

I walked past him and nodded at the girl I had seen before.

'Ciao cara,' I said to Sveva as I walked out the door.

I walked over to Umberto Salati's block of flats on Via Pestalozzi. The carabinieri cordon had gone now and I could stroll up to the outside gate without being stopped. I took out the eight keys and tried them one by one.

'What are you doing?'

I straightened up and saw a man watching me. 'I'm trying to get these keys to work,' I said.

The man looked at me with suspicion. 'Who are you?'

I evaded the question. 'I found a bunch of keys near here. I heard on the news that Umberto Salati's had been lost, so I thought I would just check here to see if they were his.'

'You found a bunch of keys? Let me have a look.'

I didn't pass them over. 'Listen, friend, I've been hired by the family to work out what really went on here.' It was stretching the truth only a little bit. The man seemed nonplussed, so I pulled out my ID.

The man stepped back and watched me trying the keys one by one. 'Mind if I try the inside door?' I asked, expecting the man to click open the outer gate. But he stood his ground, and asked to look at the keys. I couldn't see the harm and handed them over. The man looked at them one by one.

'None of these are ours,' he said. 'Try if you like.'

He pulled the gate open and I walked up to the main door. I tried all the keys but none of them worked.

I straightened up and looked at the man again. He had the sort of face that looked distrustful.

'Who lives on the ground floor this side of the building?' I asked casually.

'That'll be the Veronesi.'

'Are they in?'

'They're always in. If you want to talk to them though, I suggest you go back outside and ring their bell.'

I nodded at the man and walked back outside to the main gate. I found the Veronesi name on the buzzer. I pressed the button and an elderly voice came on.

I explained that I needed to ask him a couple of questions. The gate clicked open. By the time I was back at the inner door there was a short, bald man in slippers opening it for me.

'Come in. You'll want to know about the night Salati died? There's nothing I haven't already said to the police and the press. We came home early, ate, watched television and went to bed. Salati is five floors up. We very rarely saw him.'

'On good terms?'

'Formal niceties, nothing else.'

He had led me into a dark flat. It was in the shade of trees and balconies and felt claustrophobic. But its doors opened on to the small garden outside where Salati had been found dead. The man's wife was sitting on one of the armchairs.

'Anything else about that night?'

'Nothing.'

'But you heard him hit the ground?'

The man looked at his wife and shook his head.

'You're deep sleepers?'

'No, we're not. But we didn't hear him . . .' The woman trailed off, not wanting to describe what had happened.

'What did you hear?'

'Nothing. The rain was so loud you could barely hear anything anyway.'

The woman interrupted him. 'We heard the cat tinkling around outside.'

'How can you hear a cat?'

The man thumbed at his wife. 'She's a bird-lover and doesn't like old Jemima killing the birds. So she put a small bell on her collar to warn them off.'

'And that's all you heard? The rain and the cat?'

They both nodded.

I thanked them and walked back towards the porter's cabin at the entrance of the condominium. I don't know much about cats, because I don't like them. They're too feline for my liking, which is kind of the point of cats, I guess. But I know they don't tend to go for a stroll in the rain. I don't suppose the old couple were lying about what they heard. They were just interpreting it wrong.

The porter wasn't around, so I walked to the top of the building. Salati's flat was the last one at the end of the staircase. The door was locked and there was still police tape across the entrance.

I walked down a floor. There were four doors leading into separate flats. Presumably they all had Salati above them. I rang one bell after another but the first three didn't answer. Only the last one gave me any joy.

I introduced myself. The old woman wrapped her cardigan around herself more tightly when she heard I was investigating the death of Salati. She didn't want to talk, she said, she knew nothing about it.

I tried to talk quietly, to see how her hearing was, but she picked up on everything I said, so she seemed safe enough. I couldn't see a hearing aid wrapped around her ear at all.

'What did you hear that night?' I asked her.

'I heard him go out,' she said curtly. 'I heard his intercom sound, and out he went.'

'What sort of time?'

'I have no idea. It was late though. I was going to bed.'

'What time's that?'

'Nine-thirty.'

'How long was he out for?'

'Five minutes or so.'

'So he came back five minutes later?'

'I heard the door open again.'

'And you heard him?'

She looked like she was unsure. 'No, I didn't. But I heard the door open.'

'Don't you usually hear his footsteps above you?'

'Always, every one. He wore expensive shoes and liked to hear the heels.'

'But you didn't hear him walking around?'

'No. I didn't.'

'Wasn't that unusual?'

'I suppose so.' She looked at me with a frown. 'The other thing I heard was him pulling up his shutters.'

'Opening a window?'

'I didn't hear that, just the shutters.'

I thanked her and walked down the stairs.

It was beginning to fit together slowly. If someone had whacked Umberto Salati outside, they had come up and opened the shutters. I assumed they had opened the windows as well, though they wouldn't have made any noise. What the old woman had heard wasn't her neighbour upstairs – she didn't hear the usual heavy footsteps of an overweight man in his expensive shoes – it was his murderer.

My phone was going again. I put it to my ear and heard that superior tone again. 'Castagnetti? It's Crespi.'

'Ah.'

'I'm awaiting your report.'

'Yes,' I said slowly. It wasn't due until Monday and even then I doubted I would have anything to say. As far as I'm concerned, deadlines are like hurdles. There to be avoided, nothing else.

'The heirs of Silvia Salati's estate are anxious that you . . .'

'Which heirs are left?' I interrupted. I felt impatient and Crespi was the best person to take it out on. 'This case has proved crooked from the start.'

'How so?'

'I was under-briefed by you. Nothing you gave me last week prepared me for this.'

'I thought that was your job.'

'I'm an investigator, not a shit-stirrer. This was all shit and someone's been using me as a spoon.'

'I see it every day. The report?'

'Monday morning,' I sighed. I would have to write something. 'Though it may take longer.'

'I need it for Monday.'

'What's the rush?'

'I surely don't need to remind you of economic realities. It takes months to disinvest a deceased person's . . .'

'I get it. People want money. Who's been pushing?'

'Pardon?'

'Who wants everything wrapped up so quick?'

'I'm employed to get things done. I don't need people to press me, I press myself.'

'I'm sure you do. Let me ask you something else, Crespi. Have you got a way in to title deeds to houses, real estate records, that sort of stuff?'

'I can commission searches, certainly.'

'At this time of day?'

'It's Friday evening.'

'Let me give you some addresses and you could call one of your powerful friends.'

'I don't have powerful friends.'

'And I don't have toes. Come on, Crespi.'

'The only channels for that kind of thing at this time of day are the forces of order. They could find out with the click of a mouse.'

'And you can't?'

'I couldn't do anything until Monday.'

I gave him every address I had been to in the previous few days: the Tonin household, Sandro's flat, the di Pietro place out in Rimini, Roberta's joint in Traversetolo, Umberto's loft apartment. It was another long shot, but it needed doing. Whoever had got to Riccardo had almost certainly got to his money too. I wanted to know who was spending big in the months after his disappearance.

'I'll be round your office on Monday morning,' I said. 'You'll have everything by then?'

He grunted.

I started walking home. My whole body was aching. My ribs and right hand still hurt from the beating at the Hotel Palace. Every time I raised my voice above a whisper my ribcage seemed to protest.

I was in a foul mood. I wasn't getting anywhere and I felt like smashing something.

I've changed the way I deal with moods. When I was younger I used to walk in a straight line on busy pavements, bumping people off it. I didn't even notice I was doing it until I was older. That's when I started dealing with my little furies by attempting to drown them in *nocino* and *mirto* and any other digestif that would rot me from the inside. All that happened was that I got drunk and the furies got bigger, so I gave it up.

Nowadays I like to think I don't get black moods, but it's not true. I'm more serene on the outside, but inside I still get steamed up. The cost of serenity is deep bouts of lethargy when I can't even see the point of getting off the sofa.

I can't see the point because I know that cases like this are never conclusive. There are hints which a jury can accept or reject, but even when hints approach certainty, the courts can still be perverse. But at the moment I didn't even have many hints.

I walked home feeling exhausted. Sometimes I overdo it, go in hard on people, start punishing them because I want to punish myself. Don't ask me what for.

I suppose that's why I like my bees. I prefer their company to that of humans. They're more productive and more precise. They might sting you but they never sting each other. And I like the fact that they sting you. It means that when you start out you have to confront fear. And when you're used to it all, you still know they could get under your skin, literally. When they don't sting you're grateful for the peace, or at least the pact of non-aggression. That's all civilisation is anyway. A pact of non-aggression.

I sometimes think murder should be like a bee sting. If you do it, you die. You strike and you're out. We don't do that round here any more. Not because we don't want to, but because we want to pretend we're at peace. If you start killing people back, everything escalates. Everyone knows there's a war on then. There always is, only now everyone's got it, and they'll start tooling up, or hiding behind someone who is. So instead we pretend everything is civilised, and because we're civilised we don't kill. Not at home, anyway. We watch them, wait, eavesdrop, try to anticipate, try to read the warning signs.

I was beginning to form an idea of what had happened to Riccardo Salati. Ricky hadn't been the sentimental type. When an ageing lawyer turned up claiming to be his true father, he saw an opening.

He knew that something was secret and Tonin would probably pay to keep it that way. He didn't see a father but a pot of cash.

Ricky decided it would be an easy shake-down. He threatened to tell all to Tonin's family. He started asking for money on the quiet. Never calling it a blackmail, just a bit of help to get him through hard times. But he didn't go away. He kept coming back for more.

Ricky's train that night had been almost an hour late. And I knew enough about Ferrovie dello Stato to know that a late train always gets later. If a train is an hour late now, in half an hour it will probably be two hours late. That's the way with Ferrovie dello Stato. Ricky would have been looking around for some way to kill time. A restless type like him didn't sit in the waiting room helping old ladies with the crossword.

So he had wandered around the station looking for something to do. By chance or design, someone saw him at the station and it went from there. Someone had seen to him. Someone decided to do them all a favour.

It was pretty vague, but it seemed to fit the facts. Once Riccardo had disappeared Tonin kept his paternity hidden because he feared his family was involved. He had lost one son and didn't want to lose another. He must have guessed years ago that Sandro was involved, and that to tell the world that he, Tonin, was Riccardo's father, would lead everyone to the boy who, until then, had been his only son: Sandro.

It added up but I'm not so keen on guesses. For a 'scomparso' to become a 'presunto morto' you need more than guesses.

I turned my keys and let myself into the flat. It was freezing. The boiler must have broken again.

I took an ingot of beeswax out of a cupboard. It was thick and heavy, so I shredded it with a cheese grater into a pan. I warmed it gently, adjusting the flame so that the deep yellow lump slowly melted.

The old Salati woman's death had been a spanner in the works. She had made sure that when she died there would be one last investigation into the disappearance of her son, Ricky. Sandro had overheard about it in the office when the two receptionists had been talking about their work one Saturday morning. So Sandro decided to make the most public declaration of mourning possible and make it look like Riccardo had just been playing hide-and-seek for more than a decade. It was an amateur attempt to put us off the scent. But it was clear that old Massimo Tonin hadn't made the payment. A lawyer knows all about the documents he leaves in his wake and wouldn't be that inept. The only explanation was that the son was using the father's credit card. Nothing new about that in this city.

Then Umberto found out about his late mother's love life; he wanted it out with the Tonins. He stormed round there, to the domestic nest rather than the chilly offices of the lawyer. Salati stammered his disgust, and the Tonin woman panicked. She thought Salati knew more than he said and she called her son.

Sandro assumed his time was almost up. The only way to make sure his disposal of Ricky stayed secret was to dump Umberto. He hangs around outside the block of flats and gets impatient. He buzzes Umberto and tells him to come down, says there's a delivery, or an emergency, anything to get the man in his sights. When Umberto goes outside Sandro's on to him. He smacks Salati on the side of the head with anything he has to hand.

I put on another pan and heated up some oil I had bought in that African shop just off Viale Imbriani. The kitchen began to smell good, like suncream or something, and it made me feel better. It smelt like a childhood summer from long ago. I mixed the oil and the wax and stirred in a few spoonfuls of honey and some vanilla drops. The liquid was transparent but thick. I took it off the heat and poured it into tiny glass pots. I filled about sixty all told.

Sandro must have gone upstairs. He had seen Salati there with his body broken and had decided to go upstairs and open a door on to Salati's terrace. Make it look like a suicide and whilst he's there, check Salati hasn't done anything foolish like write a confessional. That's what the old woman heard in the flat below: Sandro pulling up shutters.

And then he makes his only mistake. He forgets to put Salati's keys somewhere. He walks out with them for some reason. Maybe his mind was elsewhere, or else he thought Salati really had written it all down and that the keys would be useful. It all came back to the keys.

Whilst the mixture was cooling it turned white, and I wrote small labels that I stuck on the lids one by one. It was satisfying work, making something beautiful and useful, doing something slowly and methodically. It was the opposite of detection, the hurried discovery of something terrible, a discovery that was useless except for the purposes of punishment or revenge.

I sat down in the armchair once I was done and tried to think about nothing. It's harder than it sounds. I tried for half an hour to think of nothing, but I kept seeing keys and Visa slips and Umberto Salati's bushy moustache caked with dry blood.

Saturday

I woke up a few hours later feeling brittle, like I could snap for lack of sleep. I looked at the clock and it was only just four in the morning. I tried to get up quietly, but every movement seemed loud and clumsy. As I walked towards the kitchen, the tendons in my left ankle clicked as I went.

The entire city was asleep. In that cold silence every thought seemed powerful and unopposed and fantasies took possession of my mind.

I sat in the armchair. I could hear traffic in the distance, hear someone's boiler firing up.

It was surprisingly noisy once you were used to the quiet. And each sound could have been any number of things.

I was thinking about what the old Veronesi couple had heard. The cat's bell, they said.

I couldn't tell if it was a dream or something real that I was remembering. Time seemed to pull apart for an instant, allowing that instant to pass in slow motion, to become something more than what it was.

I stood up and went over to the phone table where I drop my keys each night. I picked them up as silently as possible, but there was still the rattle of kissing metal. They hadn't heard the cat, I realised, but someone lifting the keys from Umberto Salati's pocket.

I slipped the keys into my jacket and counted out the eight specimen keys from Sandro Tonin's bag. I zipped them into my inside pocket and pulled the door shut.

The fog was thick but the green neon of a chemist's cross was bright. As the lines came on one by one the air seemed to turn into algae.

It was still early. I had been outside Sandro Tonin's flat since before five and there had been no movement. I was yawning every few minutes and wondering whether I should go back to bed.

At a few minutes past eight Sandro came out dressed for work. He was headed for the office by the look of his pressed trousers. I could hear the sound of his heels clicking as he walked.

Once he was out of sight I walked up to Sandro's block and quickly tried one key after another. The gate gave way. I did the same for the door on the inner courtyard and got into the building.

Inside I slipped the keys back into my pocket and started walking up the stairs. A young boy was heading out in running gear and I stopped him.

'You know which floor Sandro Tonin is on?'

'Third,' the boy said enthusiastically.

He ran off and I went up another two floors.

There were two doors on that floor. I tried the one to the right because there was an umbrella bucket outside the door with an expensive walnut wood handle poking out. That would be Sandro, I thought.

I rang the bell expecting nothing but I heard the sound of someone inside and eventually the door opened.

It was a girl. Her face was on and she had a cup of coffee in her hand.

'Sandro in?' I smiled.

'Just left,' she said sleepily.

'Who are you?' I put my good foot inside the door.

'Marzia Colombi. Who are you?'

'Renzo,' I said. I use the name so often it comes out natural by now. 'I'm a mate of Sandro's. Mind if I come in?'

I walked in without waiting for a reply and shut the door behind me. She looked at me with a mixture of scorn and terror.

'I'm not going to hurt you,' I said. I pulled out my ID.

She looked back at my face and tried to smile. 'Looks like you need a partner.'

'I don't do partners. What about you?'

'How do you mean?'

'Sandro.'

'What about him?'

'Where were you Wednesday night?'

She frowned. 'Here.'

'This where you live?'

She nodded.

'With Sandro?'

'Sure.'

'And Wednesday you were here all evening?'

'Sure.'

'And Sandro?'

She frowned. 'I don't know.'

'It's time to remember.'

'I . . .' She was about to play ignorant again, but stopped herself. 'What's all this about?'

'Did Sandro go out on Wednesday?'

She shrugged. 'He said he wanted to get some gear in.'

'What gear?'

'You know,' she said scornfully.

'Where from?'

'Lo Squarcione.'

'Who's that?'

'The guy he normally gets it from.'

'What's it, exactly?'

'Coke.'

'And Lo Squarcione sells?'

'Right.'

'Did he come back with anything on Wednesday?'

She nodded.

'And you know this character, Lo Squarcione?'

'Sure.'

'Where?'

'He hangs out around the station. Always has.'

'Dealing?'

'Doing any business he can.'

I wasn't sure what to believe. She looked too eager, like she was after something.

'What does he look like?'

'Who?'

'Sandro's dealer.'

She blinked. 'Large scar from ear to nostril. That's how he got his name I guess. He looks like the kind of kid who puts too much candy up his nose. You know, looks tense most of the time.'

I went through the flat room by room. Started emptying drawers, looking in cupboards, rifling through clothes. The girl was watching me as if she was thinking about calling for help, so I ripped the phone from its socket and threw her mobile off the balcony.

I went through the other rooms: the kitchen, the bedroom, the bathroom. There was nothing out of the ordinary. I went through the whole flat again, frustrated. It was a mess now, and the girl was whimpering. I didn't even know what I was looking for, though I had a few hopes. If I could find his father's credit card here I would be a lot happier that my theory was valid.

Nothing showed up. I pulled out my phone and called the Questura. I didn't give my name, just told them to send men round to the address. I hung up before they could ask any more questions.

I grabbed her by her upper arm and held her against the wall. 'This is a murder case, sister,' I said. 'That means people who kill and kill again. We're going to the station. Let's go and see who you see.'

She was shaking her head, staring at me with nervous eyes.

'The carabinieri will be here in a few minutes,' I said. 'I've just called them. When they get here, they'll arrest you and you'll probably spend the next ten years inside.'

'What for?' she hissed. 'What for? I haven't done anything.'

'No one ever does, do they?'

She was shaking now, not understanding my words properly, but understanding the sense somehow.

'The only way out is with me. I've told you, I'm not going to hurt you if you help me, OK? You coming or staying?'

She started crying and I put a hand under her arm, took one last look around the flat and walked out, leaving the door ajar. She leaned heavily on me as we walked down the stairs.

I threw her in the passenger seat and sat down next to her. We saw the carabinieri arrive en masse and disappear up the staircase of the block.

I started up the engine. 'You're going to wait for a bus that never comes, you got it? You see Sandro's dealer, you ask him for a cigarette. He's the only one you talk to. You don't approach anyone else, you with me? All you're doing is asking for a cigarette.'

'I'm not sure . . .'

'He tries anything and I'll put more holes in him than a scolapasta,' I said, speeding up Via Trento towards the bridge. I hardly slowed at the roundabout. I screeched round to the right and on to the forecourt. 'This may take hours,' I said, 'and it may not happen at all.' I leaned across her and opened her door. 'Just wait for that bus.'

She nodded and slammed the door shut. I parked up by the Toschi and walked back. From a few hundred metres away I could see the amassed lights of the station. Buses pulling in, heaving off. Cars dropping. Taxis hovering.

I crossed at the lights and sat on one of the stone walls

under a tree. There were a couple of Moroccan men sitting there on a rug. From here I could see her. She was taking out a cigarette from her pockets and lighting it. 'You're supposed to ask for one,' I said to myself, 'not provide your own.'

She stood in the same place for a few minutes. She glanced around all the time, but it looked like she was searching for me, not her man's man. I walked past her on the way to the ticket counter and told her to keep looking. I watched her from inside the station. Occasionally people would go up to her and ask something. She kissed a couple of people who recognised her. But she didn't ever approach anyone.

I was just walking between one window and the next when I lost her. She must have seen me disappear for an instant and was suddenly gone. I went out there immediately but couldn't spot her. There were trucks and buses parked everywhere. The Saturday morning crowds were already marching up Via Garibaldi. I ran away from the centre along the river but couldn't see her.

There was no one who even looked like her. The pavements were busy with weekend shoppers coming in from all over the province now, and it was like looking for a needle in a haystack.

I saw a girl down a side street. It wasn't Sandro's squeeze, but it looked like someone about as desperate as me. She was hovering like someone needing a score and biting her fingers like she hadn't eaten for weeks.

'You want to earn some?' I said to her.

She looked at me and assumed the obvious. 'I don't do that sort of stuff.'

She was a sorry sight. Dirty fingers and skin like a toddler's knees. Her forearms were reddened by a rash, and her joints all jutted out as if the flesh had been sucked out of her. Her eyes looked tough and dead. They moved too fast, but never seemed focussed.

'What happened to you, sweetheart?' I asked bluntly.

'How do you mean?'

'Looks like you've got something nasty on your skin.' I pointed my chin towards her forearms.

'Yeah, well . . .'

'Injecting?'

She threw her hands upwards in admission and I got a closer view of the needles' damage. I looked at her face again: if she had washed her hair since the turn of the century she could have been quite cute.

'How long have you been using?'

'A few years.' She shrugged.

'Every day?'

'Never miss one,' she said bitterly.

'Who are you buying from?' I asked.

She didn't say anything.

'With respect,' I said, 'I've had tougher assignments than shadowing a junkie.' She shrugged and I pulled out a note from my back pocket. She looked at it like a starving man might look at a plate of food.

'Lo Squarcione, right?'

She looked at me scared now. 'Who are you?' She still hadn't taken the note. She must have thought I was an undercover.

'I'm a private,' I explained.

She took the note and I told her to go find Lo

Squarcione. I didn't like paying for her habit, but I didn't suppose it made any difference. I followed her round the back of the station and within minutes she had gone up to a thirty-something man and started talking. They disappeared round a corner for a minute, just enough time to get the camera out. Someone like Lo Squarcione doesn't like to be away from the shop for too long.

He came back without the girl. He looked the opposite of the kind of dealer I'm used to. He dressed like one of the boys: a tight leather jacket and trousers with too many pockets. He could have been an undergraduate with his raffish sideburns and air of the institutionalised rebel.

I pulled my camera up to my eye and got a shot just as the man was reaching into his pocket to find a lighter. The traffic suddenly cleared and I saw his hollow cheekbones and pressed the shutter. I kept my finger down, but the traffic cut off my view again.

I looked at the shots on the screen and zoomed in on the face. Up close it was mean. The scar made him look dangerous. His black hair was gelled up and his eyes were prematurely wrinkled.

Two Moroccans under a tree were looking at me with suspicion.

'What?'

They didn't say anything.

'You selling grass?' I asked them.

They looked at me as if they hadn't understood. They were good at pretending not to understand. I held out a fifty, and nodded eagerly. Neither of them moved. They weren't going to deal in daylight to a man with a tele-photo. 'Take it,' I urged. 'You haven't seen me, OK?'

'Va bene, va bene,' one of them said, as if talking to himself.

I phoned Dall'Aglio. One of his operatives answered the phone. Eventually Dall'Aglio came on the line spit-ting blood.

'Was that you?'

'What?'

'We got an anonymous tip-off an hour or two ago. Called to a house that was turned upside down.'

'Don't be stupid,' I said quickly. 'I'm sorry I went in unauthorised, but I've got a case to wrap up from four-teen years ago. You find anything?'

'Nothing but a mess. You broke into a private dwelling and left the door open for anyone to enter.'

'I didn't break in. Sandro Tonin's partner invited me inside.'

'Really. So where is she?'

I didn't say anything.

'The defence will have a field day with your opera-tional procedure. Even if we do find something, we'll be accused of planting it. That's the problem with you privates. You're not seen as orthodox, honourable people for some reason.'

'Stop bleating. You need to find the girl. She was with me just now and was playing along, all cooperative. Gave me a story about Sandro's alibi that Wednesday night, said he had gone to see some random pusher from the station. If she was stringing me along she will have alerted him by now. She's called Marzia Colombi.'

Dall'Aglio was listening and I could hear his teeth grinding.

'Have you brought in Sandro?' I asked.

'No, not yet.'

'He's not around?'

'Left his office in a hurry minutes before we arrived.'

'He's been tipped off. Find Colombi, she'll know where he is. Something else. I've got a photograph of someone called Lo Squarcione who's come on my radar. I need a bit of background.'

'Lo Squarcione?'

'You know him?'

'Yeah, I know him,' Dall'Aglio said.

'What line's he in?'

'Delivery.'

'Of what?'

'What do you think?' The carabiniere sounded confused. 'What's Lo Squarcione got to do with this?'

'I've no idea. Is he one of yours?'

Dall'Aglio didn't say anything. Most of the petty dealers working in the open air had been picked up so many times by the carabinieri that eventually they started to get to know each other passing well.

'We know who he is,' Dall'Aglio said. 'We're watching him very closely and we don't want a poacher in the woods, you understand?'

'How long have you been watching him?' Watching was police-speak for letting Lo Squarcione lie. Letting everyone lie. It was an old habit. 'How long have you kept tabs on him?'

'Goes back years.'

'What about '95. Was he on the radar then?'

'I don't know.'

'So why don't you clear him out? He's dealing shit to every teenager this side of Reggio and you just let him carry on.'

Dall'Aglio was riled and started defending his force. 'He's one we have to leave in position.'

'Why?'

'We just do.'

'And you say us privates aren't honourable.' I felt better once I had returned the insult. Dall'Aglio wasn't going to say it out loud, but it was clear enough. Lo Squarcione must have been informing on his friends, helping police with their enquiries. If he looked tense it was because he was a squealer. It gave me a lever and I intended to use it.

I checked my gun under my armpit and watched Lo Squarcione for the next few minutes. People kept coming up to him and they would disappear off together into a block of flats and come out separately a minute later. He was making decent money, that was for sure: probably ten or twenty every five minutes.

I was about to go up to him when he walked off towards a moped. He had pulled on his helmet and sped off before I had time to take the number plate. It didn't look like he knew he was being watched. I guessed he needed a safe-house for his earnings.

I saw him head south and ran back to my car. It had a parking ticket, which I ripped off. I pulled a U-turn in front of three buses of impatient shoppers. Whatever else happened in this city, people would always buy frocks on a Saturday. Not even a war would stop it.

I caught up with Lo Squarcione as he was turning left just before the *tangenziale*. I backed off and watched the moped pull into the Blue Camel. It was a strip joint by night, one of those places where lonely men go to be reminded how lonely they are.

By day it looked like a grim building, the kind that can only look enticing under neon. The front doors were locked. I walked round the side and through an open fire door. It led into a black corridor. I couldn't see anything, and felt along the wall for a handle. I found one that led into a larger, lighter room. There were voices from the floor above and I found the stairs and walked up quietly.

I saw him at the far end of the room flanked by a couple of heavies.

'Squarcione!' I shouted like an old buddy.

I sat down opposite him but the two men were immediately at my elbows.

'What do you want?' One of the bruisers said, pulling me up hard by my hair. He was a shaven-headed nut with a thick nose.

'I want a word with Squarcione,' I said.

He was watching the scene.

The other thug whispered in Lo Squarcione's ear. Lo Squarcione pointed at a chair opposite.

I leaned over the table as the bruisers retreated.

'Lo Squarcione?'

'Who wants to know?'

'Castagnetti.'

'Who are you?'

'Private investigator.'

'I'm not hiring.'

'I'm already hired. And you've come on to my radar.'

Lo Squarcione looked at me and his sneer froze. He seemed more dangerous up close. The scar made him look like a street fighter. 'Any radar that's got me on the screen is nearing the end of its useful life.'

I was cheered by his arrogance. It's always a reflection of fear.

'But, you see, you're already on my radar. I want help getting questions answered.'

'I'm not taking questions, the interview's over.'

He held his hand beside his shoulder and bent his fingers forwards. The heavies behind him jumped towards me.

'There's a lot in it for you.' I had to speak quickly. 'I'm investigating something from fourteen years back. You're not in the frame because you were still in nappies back then.'

Lo Squarcione stopped the bruisers by raising his fingers.

'What', he said through dark teeth, 'is in it?'

'Glory.'

'Not interested.'

'Money. There's an inheritance involved.'

'Whose?'

'A man. Two men.'

Lo Squarcione looked at me with interest.

'How much?'

'I will have to talk to the men's descendants. They're in a position to approve a reward for information leading to a satisfactory resolution of the case.'

'Hundred thousand.'

I showed him my palms as if to say I was powerless. 'I'll talk to them.'

'And what do I have to do?'

'Answer questions with whatever honesty you've got left. I want to know about a deal you did recently.'

He smiled, like he had gone back to being a boy.

'What's so funny?' I asked.

'You know how many deals I do in a night?' He dropped the smile.

The arrogance was beginning to try my patience now and I suddenly felt tense. 'All I know about you is that you shovel shit to children . . .'

'Don't be rude,' he said coolly. 'What's the difference between me and that drinks dispenser over there. I'm just giving them what they want.'

'What did you give Sandro Tonin?'

'Who?'

'Sandro Tonin. He came your way to score on Wednesday night.'

'Means nothing to me. Anyway, they all use nicknames.'

'Here.' I pulled the photograph of Sandro out of my pocket and tossed it across to him. 'This is what he looks like. There's a man been murdered', I gunned, 'and I don't know why your name keeps coming up.'

'Who's been murdered?' He was trying to follow.

I ignored the question. 'Did you see this man on Wednesday night?'

The man shook his head. He looked at me with that arrogant look again, shaking his head to say he didn't answer questions.

'If Lo Squarcione was in the witness stand,' I stared at the ceiling, trying to aim my question to the heavies behind me, 'would people believe him?'

'What are you talking about?' Lo Squarcione spat.

'Just thinking aloud. Drug-dealers don't normally make good witnesses. People seem to think they're rotten, and I'm inclined to agree. But in his case . . .'

'You saying I'm a grass?'

'You said that. I wouldn't ever say that.'

An elbow hit me above the ear and the pain shot through my shoulder.

The information was worth the blow. Lo Squarcione was a squealer all right. The guilty always leap to defend their honour because it's the only way they can make it look like they've got any honour left. Lo Squarcione was a grass, and that meant he would normally sing from whatever songsheet he was given. That's what grasses were like. They said anything if it made them some money or bought some protection.

I leaned across the table and whispered. He had to lean close to hear my words. 'I know you're a squealer. My friends in the Questura told me all about you. Unless you set me straight about this Sandro piece of shit, I'll tell everyone in the city that you do the uniform's dirty work for them, you with me?'

He had gone a pleasing shade of white.

'Wednesday night,' I said slowly, 'did you see Sandro Tonin?'

He looked at me with disdain. 'What am I supposed to say?' he asked. That was typical. The idea of the truth was so alien to him that he wanted me to tell him what I wanted to hear. That's what grasses are like.

'This is one of your regulars. You know him well enough. Just tell me if you saw him on Wednesday night.'

He looked at me and shrugged. 'Sure, I saw him.'

'Do you ever tell the truth?'

Lo Squarcione shrugged again, like he didn't know what he had done. It looked to me like he was the kind of cuckold who gave away alibis like he gave out his poisons: he probably sold them to the highest bidder.

'You saw this boy on Wednesday night? What time?'

'How do I know?'

'You're sure you're telling this right? You saw Sandro Tonin on Wednesday night did you?' I asked uncertain.

'I saw him,' he said, trying to sound convincing.

I got up to leave. 'I'll let you know about that reward,' I said.

I walked out frustrated. It felt instinctively that my guesses from last night were all wrong. It might have been true that Sandro had been with his woman all evening, and had only gone out to score some substance to pickle his brain. You didn't need to be a genius to know that a guilty man needing to set up a watertight alibi wouldn't exactly ask Lo Squarcione for one.

In the car I took snaps of all the number plates in the Blue Camel car park just for luck. I drove off thinking about Lo Squarcione. I assumed he was simply pond life, a peddler of unpleasantries. It was possible that he was with the nice gentlemen of the south, but that seemed unlikely. Informers from that part of the world tend to be used for building foundations. Lo Squarcione's accent was from round here. This was a local racket run by amateurs. Not that that made him any less dangerous. He would certainly have decent backup. But it meant Lo Squarcione almost certainly couldn't count on what euphemistically used to be called political assistance.

It was yet another dead end. Sandro had seemed a likely bet and now I had lost another twenty-four hours. It didn't seem much set against fourteen years, but it was only days since Umberto Salati had been killed. Every hour counted. As soon as normality returned and the momentum was lost, nothing would stand out any more. I needed to understand what had happened Wednesday night but nothing was connecting.

The lack of sleep was getting to me. My concentration was evaporating now the adrenalin of the chase had gone. I yawned and felt my jaw ache. I tried to think about the case, but my mind had the staying power of a leaf in autumn.

I parked on Viale Mentana and walked to my flat. There was nothing to do but sit and think.

I looked at the bee balm I had put into tiny containers last night. They were properly set now. I checked for lumps but it looked smooth and white. I unscrewed a cap and ran my finger across the top of the oily mixture. It smelt as you would expect: vanilla, coconut, the usual. I rubbed it off my finger and screwed the top back on.

I sat on the sofa and thought about old Massimo Tonin. I couldn't believe it was him. He didn't seem the type. There was no motive. I didn't even think he had paid for that mourning notice, though I was sure he knew who had.

His son Sandro had seemed plausible, but before I had even got to him, it felt wrong. Dall'Aglio would bring him in anyway, and they might find something in his flat, but Sandro had been more concerned about buying his fix than silencing the past. His mother had phoned him, that I knew. But it might just have been, as Dall'Aglio said, a mother phoning her son.

I thought about that. They were talking when I got there on Wednesday. They had been talking on the phone as soon as Umberto Salati had left. I made a note to ask Infostrada how long that little chat had lasted. The only bit I had heard was the end of their chat, when old Tonin and I went in. 'I'll call you back,' she had said.

I'll call you back, I said to myself. The woman had said it to her son. But there had been only one call. That's what Dall'Aglio had told me.

It probably wasn't anything. We all say stuff we never do. But she hadn't called him back, and mothers normally do. They do everything for their children, especially if there's only one. They do everything, I repeated, trying to think of all the absurd things my friends allowed their mothers to do. Their ironing, their cooking, their cleaning.

Someone had told me that the Tonin woman made Sandro's bed and put food in his fridge. It was that receptionist who had said it. Said that the mother came into town to do all his chores.

That was when the penny dropped. How did the woman get around? I kept imagining her stuck in the Tonin villa all day because that's where I had always seen her. But she spent half her time in the city by the sound of it. Old Tonin had made out his wife was immobile, but it sounded like she got around just fine.

It was late afternoon by now. It was dull outside, the grey turning black. I called the Studio Tonin, but there was no reply.

I called Crespi's phone. 'I need Giovanna Monti's number.'

'My assistant? Why?'

'I just do. Where is she?'

'She left at lunchtime, always does on a Saturday.'

'What's her mobile?'

He gave me her number.

'Any news on those properties?' I asked impatiently.

'I'm engaged in other matters this afternoon. I'll look into it on Monday. What time are you coming round?'

'When I'm ready.'

I phoned Monti and asked for Serena's number. She asked me why and I said it was to do with a murder. That put her straight and she gave me the number just to get shot of me.

I dialled the number.

'Sì.'

'Serena? Castagnetti.'

'What now?'

'I need to ask you just one or two more questions.'

'Now?'

I listened to the background noise, hoping that I wouldn't hear a man in the background. 'You busy?'

'I'm about to meet friends.'

'It will only take two minutes,' I said. 'Where are you?'

'Bruno's.'

'Stay there. I'll be round in a minute.'

I gathered my stuff quickly. I opened up my bag and checked the contents. The camera was in there. A bit of cash, eight keys, the notebook, the cuffs. I put the pistol in place under my arm and looked around the flat. I picked up a tub of the balm and put it in a pocket.

She was there waiting for me when I walked up to the bar. Bruno's is a noisy bar at this time on a Saturday. People were raising glasses, laughing hard, shouting at friends on the street. Serena looked even better than I remembered her. She had changed her clothes since leaving the office, and was dressed to go out for the evening. She was unbuttoned at the front, and it was hard not to admire her.

'What is it now?' she said.

'You said something the other day.'

'What?'

'You said Sandro's mother came in to make his bed, fill his fridge.'

'Did I?' she said.

'I just wondered . . . are you sure about that?'

She laughed nervously. She looked less innocent then. She must have seen what I was thinking because she blushed.

'You had a thing with Sandro?'

'It wasn't even a thing.'

That's what I mean when I said this city was small. There's never more than one degree of separation. 'It's irrelevant what it was,' I said. 'I just want you to be sure about what you're telling me. You said Teresa Tonin would go to his flat to make his bed and so on.'

'Sure.'

'Certain?'

She nodded like she had been responsible for messing up the bed. It wasn't an image I wanted to linger on.

'How did she get into town if she doesn't drive?'

'I don't know.'

'Did she often come in?'

She shrugged.

'OK, thanks.'

She looked at me. I thought she was about to give an explanation for something, but she just asked if that was it. I said it was and she walked off.

I called after her, remembering the bee balm. 'Here, take this.'

She turned round and looked at me and then at the tub.

'What's that?'

'It's a kind of balm,' I said. 'Cures all ailments known to man. I make it from beeswax.'

She looked at me and didn't know what to do. She took it out of my hand and unscrewed the lid. She smelt it and ran a finger around the surface and looked at it. She wiped it on to her lips. 'He let me stay in his flat once or twice, that's all,' she said.

'I don't need to know,' I said, unsure why she was trying to prove her innocence to me.

'It's just you seemed to think . . .'

'I'm thinking about other things right now.'

I went back to Borgo delle Colonne and picked up the car. I drove back to La Bassa one last time. I parked in the main square in Sissa and looked around. You couldn't see further than your nose the fog was so thick, but it meant that voices carried. I could hear the distant shrieks of teenagers. I could hear the old ladies incanting in the church. I walked around the square and saw a bar with little lights strung from one corner to another. Here and there they were hung too low and people had to duck to get in. There seemed to be a pensioners' dance going on. The music was oompah *liscio*, but very gentle and quick, so that some of the smoothies looked snappy and sharp. The bar was three deep with men buying *amari* and beer.

I wandered around for a few minutes, listening to the sounds of Saturday night in a village in winter. I kept thinking about Teresa Tonin, wondering how she got about. I returned to the car and drove on to the Tonin estate. When I got there all the lights were off and the gate was closed.

I needed to get in unannounced, so I parked further up the road and went in on foot.

As soon as I had landed the other side of the railings a dog started barking. It didn't sound like it was getting closer, but it was going nuts, gnashing and growling somewhere in the distance.

The Tonin place was all in darkness, but the lodge off to the right had lights on. As I walked towards it I guessed this was where the dog was. It was a small cottage with a tidy pile of logs stacked outside.

I rang the bell. The dog kept up his performance and I heard a gruff voice inside telling him to shut up.

The door opened and I saw an old woman I hadn't seen before. She had the suspicion of a peasant, and held the dog in front of her to remind me who was in charge.

'Is this where the gardener lives? I'm a friend of the Tonin family. You might have heard Massimo Tonin is in some trouble, and I need to see . . . I'm sorry, I've forgotten his name.'

'Giulio. Giulio Bocchialini.'

'You're his wife?'

She nodded, pulling the dog back from my groin. She was a large woman with soft hair growing around her jawline.

'Who is it?' A voice shouted from inside.

'Was your husband at home on Wednesday night?' I asked quickly. She didn't have time to reply when he appeared at her shoulder. It was the gardener I had seen a few days ago. I didn't know if he had heard the question, but he looked at me with wide, blue eyes.

'What is it?'

'I need to ask you a couple of questions,' I said.

'What are you after?'

'Do you drive as well as garden?'

'What do you mean?'

228

'Did you drive Teresa Tonin into the city on Wednesday night?'

He didn't answer.

I repeated the question. The man looked at me with contempt.

'What do you want exactly?'

'Did you?'

He shook his head, but he had lost his self-assurance.

'Who did you drive?'

He didn't say anything, so I reached for my phone and dialled Dall'Aglio's number.

The man put a thin hand on my wrist and stared at me. 'Who are you calling?'

'The carabinieri.' I let the phone ring on until he started talking.

'Hold it,' he said quickly. I stopped the call to the Questura, but he didn't say anything else. I was about to redial when he started his little confession. 'I've been doing the same thing for forty years. It's simple, honest, humble work. I fix their boiler. I sweep the leaves. I change their tyres. I queue at the post-office.' He was saying it with glazed eyes, like he had just gone into retirement and he was missing it already.

'And did you drive the woman into the city on Wednesday night?'

He looked at me. Whatever he was thinking, one thing was clear: he knew why I was asking. His face appeared old suddenly, and his eyes opened wide like he had just seen his last minute of freedom flash in front of him.

'Wait here a minute,' he said, walking inside his house

at a brisk pace. I followed him. The TV was on loud in a dark room.

I followed him into a small garage. I looked round at the chaos. Boxes stuffed with old tiles and taps and odd nuts. There were rags and ancient copies of gardening magazines. There wasn't anything that stood out. Certainly not a pair of keys.

Before I knew what was happening I heard an explosion. I found myself doubled up, almost on the floor on instinct. It can't have been more than a metre or two from me and my ears were ringing.

I reached for my gun as I crouched there, but the room was horribly still. I stood up. The gardener was on the floor. His face all intact, but there was nothing behind it. It looked like a mask floating in a lake.

You couldn't see an entry point for a bullet but the exit was pretty clear. He was missing the back of his brain. There was a line of blood and cartilage up the wall.

The woman came rushing in with the barking hound. She screamed when she saw her husband and looked at me.

'He took his life. I didn't even know he had a gun.'

She was screaming and wailing. I wasn't sure she had heard what I had said. I tried to get my phone out to finish that call to the Questura. That's what I should have done two minutes ago and then perhaps this man would still be alive. Two minutes ago he had been a walking, talking human being and now he was cooling matter, nothing more. I could still hear the sound of blood and cartilage falling from the walls to the ground.

The woman must have let go of the dog because it jumped for me, its paws at head height. It knocked me backwards and fell on top of me, its teeth going for my neck. I got my thumbs into the soft bit of his throat and squeezed with everything I had. I managed to hold his gnawing teeth away from me until he started whimpering.

'Pull it off,' I shouted at the woman but she didn't move. She had frozen. I shouted again, but by then the dog was almost gone and I rolled over on top of it and relaxed my grip. It lay there coughing and whining.

I took out my phone. 'Get Dall'Aglio. It's an emergency,' I said.

Dall'Aglio came on the line.

'The Tonins' fixer has topped himself.'

'What?'

'The gardener on their estate. He just swallowed a speeding bullet.'

'Where?'

'In the grounds, round the back.'

'I'll be there right away.'

I looked at the woman. She was staring into space and shaking. I took her into the room with the TV on and sat her down. She didn't seem able to focus on anything.

'Why did he do it?'

She looked at me with eyes so sharp they could have sliced bread. She didn't say anything, but it was pretty clear from her face that she thought I was part of the answer.

'I was questioning him about Wednesday night,' I said. 'I was asking if he was at home.' She was staring at the TV and I could see its bright lights reflected in her pallid flesh. 'Was he?'

She shook her head.

'Where did he go?'

She was still shaking her head. I wasn't sure if she wasn't saying or didn't know.

'Did he often up and leave?'

She shrugged.

'How long was he gone for?'

She just managed to whisper her reply. 'About an hour.'

I sat there with her whilst we waited for Dall'Aglio and his men. He arrived within a few minutes. One of his officers took the woman away. Others went into the garage and started photographing the corpse.

Dall'Aglio was staring at me like he blamed me for everything bad that had happened in his life.

'Why can't you just do things by the book?' he asked.

'That's the best thing about my job, there is no book.'

'Why is it that wherever you go, people start dying?'

'This time it *was* suicide,' I said. 'Bocchialini and that Tonin woman were in it together. I had half an idea, listening to Bocchialini talk, that he was involved with the Tonin woman himself.'

'Why?'

'He was listing all the menial chores he used to do for the family like he was restoring the Sistine Chapel. He loved something in that household, and I don't think it was his salary or his overalls.'

'You think he and Teresa . . . ?'

'Not my taste, possibly not yours,' I conceded, 'but love works in mysterious ways. If they were an item and Sandro was their son, it might make the whole thing a lot more comprehensible.'

Dall'Aglio was frowning. It was just an idea of mine, but it was one of those that seemed to make sense retrospectively. It didn't matter whether it was true or not for now.

We stood there like an embittered couple, unable to separate because we couldn't get by without the other. We knew we had both been stupid and didn't want to talk for fear of revealing the fact. He thought I was reckless. I thought he was passive.

For once I thought he might be right. Since Monday, there had been two fresh corpses and I knew it was my interfering which had, in some ways, produced them. That, Dall'Aglio would tell me, was why the police tactic was sometimes to watch instead of act. I had rushed in as usual, and now one of the suspects, Bocchialini, was as much use to us as a sieve in a flood. We stood there continuing the argument in silence, watching the men measuring up the body.

'Come on,' he said eventually, 'let's go and find the Tonin woman.'

We went into the main house. The door was open but everything was in darkness. She must have known we were coming because she was standing halfway down the stairs.

'You heard about Bocchialini?' I asked.

'What?' She looked up sharply.

'He just swallowed a bullet. Put his grey matter all over your garden tools.'

She had her mouth wide open and was holding both hands over it. Her fingers eventually went on to her lower teeth as if trying to open her mouth still wider. I figured, given that reaction, he had been more than her gardener and chauffeur.

'That's one trigger you didn't pull,' I said, wanting to kick her whilst she was down. 'My carabinieri colleagues are getting very impatient.'

I smiled at her. She was staring at us, but she was rubbing her hair into a mess.

We started walking up the stairs towards her. 'It's all over now,' Dall'Aglio said. 'It's finished.'

She didn't say anything.

'Let me tell you how it happened,' I said, 'and you tell me when I go wrong.' She was looking beyond us at the armed officers who were standing at the bottom of the stairs a few metres below us. 'Back in '95 your husband told you about his fling with the Salati woman. Told you about Riccardo. That was a hard hit to take, but there was worse. Young Ricky was bleeding your husband dry and you didn't like the look of it. Call it blackmail, or guilt money, or whatever, that boy was costing your family millions. The last straw was when your unfaithful husband gave his bastard son a brick of cash on San Giovanni.'

She didn't say anything.

'You told Bocchialini to go and pick Riccardo Salati up from the station. Someone carrying eighty-five million lire or whatever it was doesn't want to hang around a station. His train was late and the cost of a ride to Rimini would have seemed like peanuts.' I stopped and looked at her. She was shaking her head. 'Bocchialini picked him up and you sat in the back of the car and strung his windpipe. You took him some place and buried him. An unmarked grave for the bastard. What was it? The river Po?'

'You don't know what you're talking about.'

I looked at her. 'You and Bocchialini had something going on. It wouldn't surprise me if Sandro was his son.'

'That's your fantasy, is it?'

I watched her close and she looked like she was waking up from a fantasy of her own. You could see it in the smug way she smiled, the way she pulled her clothes around her as if becoming aware for the first time that she was a performer, acting out a role she had written herself.

'So you dumped him somewhere and thought nothing more of it. Life went on. No one suspected you. No one even suspected your family. But then last Friday Silvia Salati dies and leaves a will. She hires me. She wants the whole case reopened. You hear about it on the grapevine, because your son heard about it in his office on Saturday. He told you that a private dick was on the case. So you panicked and placed a mourning notice in *La Gazzetta*. Only you pay with your husband's card and not in cash. That's not the kind of mistake a lawyer would ever make.'

She was trying to force a smile, but it had melted on her face and she looked strained, like smiling was the last thing she could do. 'You haven't got any evidence for any of this.' She wasn't denying it any more, just challenging me to prove it.

'On Wednesday,' I went on, 'when Umberto finds out his brother Riccardo was from your side of the fence, he works something out. His little brother wasn't the sort to get all emotional about a long-lost father. Riccardo was the sort who would ask for a loan before asking for a hug. Umberto realised that Ricky would have been round to yours asking for cash pretty quickly. And he was right, wasn't he? On Wednesday Umberto worked out what Riccardo must have been doing. He knew who would have wanted him out the way, and started leaning on you. There was only one thing to do. Send him the same place as his brother Riccardo.'

Her eyes were closed now, like she was concentrating. She was shaking her head vigorously in denial.

'You rang his bell, got him to come down into the courtyard, and you hit him hard with something from Bocchialini's shed. Or maybe he was down there anyway, standing outside in the courtyard having a cigarette. Once you've rearranged his skull, you decide to go upstairs to open the window to make it look like suicide, only then you have his keys in your pocket. I thought it was your son Sandro when I woke up this morning, but I realised it couldn't be him. Not just because he's a no-hoper junkie who only thinks about scoring Colombian sherbet. It couldn't have been him because he wears expensive shoes which make a noise when he walks. The woman below Salati's flat didn't hear a thing. It must have been a short, slim person, probably a woman.'

I had wound her up so much she was wagging her finger at me. 'You don't know anything about it.' Her face looked much older when not made up. There were vertical wrinkles on her upper lip.

Dall'Aglio had been watching the whole scene and now stepped forward to read her her rights. One of his men clicked the bracelets on her.

'You'll have to come to the Questura too,' Dall'Aglio said to me. 'We'll need a statement.'

I drove there in a daze. It was well beyond midnight, but the streets of the city were busy with kids out on the town, revving their mopeds and showing off their new clothes.

Dall'Aglio took me down into the basement where they had the interview rooms. It was cold and damp and a bare light bulb hung from the ceiling on a frayed wire. He and another officer listened to everything I said like I was under suspicion myself. They took me through the whole week, asking me to repeat everything time and again.

Dall'Aglio didn't seem in the mood to take advice from me, but when the statement was all printed up and signed, I told him to follow the money.

'When Riccardo went missing,' I told him, 'he was carrying a large sum in cash.'

'So?'

'Whoever clocked Riccardo Salati had a tidy sum to invest. Look into Teresa Tonin and Giulio Bocchialini's finances from back then. You'll find something. Something will come up.'

He looked at me like there was no trust left. There was a knock at the door.

'Sir?' A young man came in. 'Lieutenant Bollani wanted you to see this. That man we arrested this afternoon, Sandro Tonin ... he had this inside his wallet.'

He passed Dall'Aglio a transparent plastic bag. Inside was a credit card. Dall'Aglio held the top of the bag and twisted it so that he could see the name of the card. 'Massimo Tonin,' he read.

'I forgot to tell you,' I said. 'Sandro was using his father's credit card. He phoned in the mourning notice on Sunday. Check his phone records and I'll lay a bet with you that he called our dear *Gazzetta*.'

'OK.' Dall'Aglio flicked the boy out of the room with his fingers.

'He was using his father's card,' I said, staring at Dall'Aglio. 'He paid for the mourning notice. It wasn't anything to do with Massimo Tonin. Only having already lost one son, Tonin didn't want to lead the police to another, so he didn't say anything about it.'

Dall'Aglio looked across at me and raised his eyebrows. 'Doesn't make Sandro a murderer.'

'You were pretty keen to charge old Tonin when you thought he had done it.'

'He was keeping secrets, that made me suspicious.'

'Well, that mourning notice has been a distraction from the start.'

'That's why it was placed, I suppose,' said Dall'Aglio. 'Time for a little interrogation,' he said, standing up. It was his way of dismissing me.

I walked out into the corridor. Even at this time of night there were dozens of officers walking briskly from one room to the next.

There was a coffee machine at one end of the corridor. I dropped a coin in the slot and listened to the strange whirring as a white, plastic thimble dropped into metallic fists and filled with the steaming black liquid they were passing off as coffee.

I could feel disappointment come over me like mud. I felt suddenly heavy. I liked conclusions and this was only the pretence of one. I seemed to have resolved a case that was incidental to Riccardo's disappearance. Everything pointed to Teresa Tonin and yet there seemed nothing that could connect her to Riccardo's vanishing act. I hadn't even resolved what I had been commissioned to do in the first place: to certify whether Riccardo was dead or alive.

I had hoped that all the loose ends of the case could be resolved, everything wrapped up by a culprit's proud confession. Instead, I was left to speculate about everything that we didn't know. We still had no murder weapon for Umberto and no body for Riccardo. Kind of made a conviction difficult, if not impossible. All we had was a pile-up of probabilities. The evidence was about as hard as butter on a beach.

That meant that soon enough the press would start to listen to Teresa Tonin's side of the story. The pendulum of public opinion would swing behind the poor mother. She would hire a lawyer, maybe even her husband, to *insabbiare*. It happened all the time around these parts. Contradictory evidence would turn up in unexpected places. Investigating magistrates were dropped from a case because of some stitch-up. Whispering campaigns cast enough doubts to make even a hot gun unreliable. The obvious got silted up with the decoy, until the decoy became the story and the obvious walked free. That's what Italian justice is all about.

It was the middle of the night and I was just about to walk out the back door when I caught a glimpse of the gardener's widow. She was sitting in a chair with a female officer next to her. She was still shaking and staring into space.

I walked up to them. The widow looked at me like she still believed I had pulled the trigger.

'Excuse me,' I said. The female officer straightened up. 'Could I ask something?'

They both just looked at me.

'How long had your husband worked for the Tonins?'

'Thirty years.'

'That right?'

She nodded.

'Did you resent the time your husband spent at Tonin's house?'

'What's that supposed to mean?'

'Do you think he went beyond the call of duty?'

She held my stare. 'He was always on duty. That's what it's like when you're domestics. You live on the job. We've lived in their grounds all our married life. And now, when they find themselves in trouble, it's Giulio who dies.'

I nodded slowly, trying to show her that I shared her indignation. 'Where was your husband from?' I asked.

'His family were all from near Borgotaro.'

'Up in the hills?'

'Sure. His mother owned a small farm up there.'

'What about his father?'

'Died in the war.'

'Where's the farm exactly?'

'What's it to you?' She said it without malice.

'Where is it?' I repeated.

'Just beyond the bridge on the left. He sold it when his mother died.'

'When?'

'A few years ago.'

'What was it called?'

'Il Mulino.'

I looked at her. She replied so absent-mindedly that she must have thought I was just passing the time of night. She hadn't put anything together yet, had no idea quite who her husband had been.

Dall'Aglio was still at his desk at 4 a.m. That's what I liked about him. He worked my hours. I knew what I needed but he wouldn't like it.

'Listen,' I said to him as he finally put down the receiver, 'there's been a lot of blood spilt. Two lives lost, maybe three. I still need to resolve the Riccardo Salati case and I'm going to ask you something unusual. I need a dozen men.'

He laughed.

'Your chance to be a hero,' I said.

'Why do I get the impression that's a role you want for yourself?'

'That's bull. Nothing I want less, I assure you. I'm not the one with medals.'

He patted his chest and looked at me with a smile. He liked the idea of being a hero. There aren't many people who don't. He wanted to walk halfway down those front steps and tell the doubting media that he had an incredible story from fourteen years ago that all his predecessors had failed to crack.

'When?' He looked at me with resignation.

'Tomorrow morning.'

'It's morning already.'

He agreed in the end. He took more convincing than a nun in a nightclub, but eventually he sighed and said OK. He said the order would go out as soon as the new shift came on at 8 a.m.

I walked home exhausted. I sat in the flat trying to think things through, but I was too tired. The flat was a mess and I couldn't even cook something to eat because the pans were full of dried beeswax and oil. A week's worth of washing-up was balanced in the sink like a cartoon, two columns rising to shoulder height.

I must have been thinking about my bees, because I suddenly realised that families in Italy are just like hives. It's where the woman rules. She rules because she's a mother, and she never retires. She fights for her children until the death, and – in Silvia Salati's case – beyond it.

Sunday

I slept until mid-morning. When I finally got out of bed I saw something I hadn't seen for weeks. The sun was out and the sky was a dark blue. It was as if the thick, cloying fog of winter had opened up and decided to allow us one blissful reminder of what it would be like when the spring really arrived. Out of my window I could see the cupolas of the city skyline looking plump and august. It felt like I had rediscovered old friends.

After breakfast I got in the car and drove through the city. It was unrecognisable. People were sitting out and taking their coffees in the bright cold. Instead of selling umbrellas to damp pedestrians, immigrants were now selling sunglasses and pirate CDs on flat cardboard. Cigarette smoke spiralled in the sun. The *trattorie*, which had been eerily quiet all week, now sounded their atonal percussion of cutlery and cork-screws as they got ready for the Sunday trade. The bellowing joviality was back in full swing.

I drove out to Borgotaro. It didn't take long.

The day seemed even more magnificent up there. People were walking around the bars. Most were wearing dark glasses. You could see the mountains, their peaks only a little higher than where you were standing, their snow glistening like *fior di latte*.

The *pasticcerie* were doing a roaring trade, piling dozens of bite-size puffs on to rectangular trays. I looked around the place and saw fur and ribbons and the glint of wine glasses being refilled. It felt like the typical, affluent Sunday morning in the sun. People were even buying ice-cream. Polystyrene baths were being filled with seedy crimson sorbets and pale, shiny creams.

I found Il Mulino easily enough. The farmer and his wife were standing around. They looked horrified at the number of uniforms crawling all over their land. I watched the cadets with their trowels. They were lined up like toy soldiers and worked north to south, then east to west, micro-ploughing the soil.

The mess, the farmer must have known, would be nothing compared to the publicity. He might already have an idea what they were looking for. The carabinieri don't normally plough your field to sow corn, he knew that. He could see the value of his land collapsing before his eyes. Human remains don't normally add much to the value of your pasture.

I spoke to the commanding officer, one of the uniforms who used to make Dall'Aglio's coffee only a year ago. He was so young I couldn't help being condescending.

'Ask the locals about any caves, ravines, rivers, wells, woods.'

'I know what I'm doing,' he said, defensively.

'Ask about any place old Bocchialini might have known, places he used to go to. Clubs he used to belong to.'

He shouted something to one of his men to make sure that I knew he wasn't listening any more.

'Who have you interviewed?' I asked.

He didn't say anything, which I took to mean he hadn't spoken to anyone. I walked away, heading towards the farmhouse where I could see the farmer with his hands on his hips.

The officer called me back. 'This is being treated as a crime scene,' he shouted.

'No entry?'

'None.'

I walked back towards him and tried to keep calm. 'I'm practically in charge of this investigation. I wouldn't say Dall'Aglio's taking orders from me, but he's taking advice, you with me?'

The man looked at me like I had urinated on his shoes.

I set off towards the farmer again and the officer ignored me.

'You know anything about this?' I said to the farmer.

He shook his head.

'They haven't told you what they're looking for?'

He shook his head again.

'You don't know what this is about?'

He didn't like that many questions, and spat something out of his mouth on to the path.

We watched the men coming and going, bringing samples of this or that to the commanding officer. 'They'll leave this place tidier than when they arrived,' I joked to the farmer, who only grimaced unhappily.

I told him what they were looking for and he just nodded with his eyes closed.

'Looks like good land,' I started, trying to engage

him. I gave him my card and told him to give me a call if he ever needed help of any kind.

'This you?' he said, reading the card.

I walked back to the car. There wasn't anything I could do but watch. I tried to talk to some of the combers, but no one would say anything.

I phoned Lo Bue.

'Lo Bue?'

'Speaking.'

'It's Castagnetti, I had an enjoyable stay at your hotel a few days ago if you remember.'

'What do you want?'

'I might have your man.'

'Meaning?'

'Or woman. We think we know what happened to Riccardo Salati.'

'And?'

'He's dead.'

'And his purse?'

Lo Bue would have ripped pearls out of a woman's ears if they were worth it.

'We don't know yet. We don't even have the body. But we think we know what happened.'

'Who did it?'

'One's dead, the other's inside.'

'So?'

'You were right. Riccardo had money on him at the time. Eighty-five million. He really was about to pay his debts.'

'Who took it?'

'My bet would be with the guy that's dead.'

'What are you talking about? Who took his money?'

'Like I said, the guy who's dead might have pocketed it, might have been the woman.'

I laughed. Trying his patience was my only revenge for the kicking he had served up. I would rather have kicked him back but you couldn't do that to a Calabrian hotel manager.

'I'll give you the number of the notary dealing with the case. I'm sure he'll be helpful. His name's Crespi.'

I hung up. I didn't like dealing with him but you couldn't get anything done here unless you cut deals. It was as if you had to ask permission from the underworld to go after the loose cannon criminals. Lo Bue might be useful to me in the future and I was sure Crespi was man enough to know how to deal with his sort. He probably was his sort, for all I knew.

I tried to call Tonin on his phone but it was permanently off. He had probably had journalists and friends calling him all morning, and he had given up answering.

It took under an hour to get to his house. The gate was as foreboding as ever. There were a couple of photographers hanging around outside. They said they had been ringing the intercom all morning with no joy.

I walked up to the thing and held the buzzer for long enough to appear rude again. No answer. I rang again, holding the buzzer for a good ten seconds.

'Who is it?'

'Castagnetti.'

'Haven't you had enough?'

'Not quite. There are a few loose ends, and you're one of them.'

'Meaning?'

'I thought it only polite to tell Elisabetta of her father's fate in person. Before she reads it in my report or, more probably, in the papers. I'm driving there now.'

'So?'

'I wondered if you wanted to come.'

The line went quiet. It would have sounded like he was laughing, but the pauses between breaths were too long. It sounded like he was shuddering plenty of tears. I felt almost sorry for the man. The carabinieri had arrested his wife and were searching for his son's body. His other son, the man he thought was his son, was probably another man's. The girl in Rimini was the last thing he had left in the world.

We didn't talk until we were past Bologna. After an hour of silence I started making small talk, asking about his favourite food. He replied almost absent-mindedly, telling me about how he loved seafood, how his parents were from near Venice and used to cook anything they pulled out of the sea.

'My favourite', I said, watching the road disappear underneath us, 'is cotolette. When I was growing up I spent some time with my aunt and uncle, and she used to make the most incredible cotolette.'

'Veal or pork?' he asked.

'Veal,' I said, as if it were obvious. 'Do you like coto-lette?' I turned to look at him but he was staring ahead, narrowing his eyes.

He must have realised where I was going because he sighed as if I were forcing him to betray his wife one last time.

'Did your wife ever make cotolette?' I asked gently.

'She did,' he said formally, like he was already in court.

'Traditional way?' I asked. 'Flour, egg and bread-crumbs?'

'Sure,' he said. 'And a bit of lemon.'

'And how did she thin out the fillets?'

I turned to look at him quickly. He had closed his eyes. 'The usual way,' he whispered. 'She uses a batti-carne.'

'OK,' I said, trying to make it easier. 'It might be nothing.'

The batticarne was the size of an auctioneer's gavel. It was the little metallic hammer used to thin out meat. One side was usually smooth and the other slightly spiked.

We didn't speak again until we got to Via dei Caduti. I left Tonin in the car and walked up to the palazzo.

'Who is it?' said a young voice when I had rung the buzzer.

'Elisabetta? It's Castagnetti.'

'No one's in,' she said.

'I came to see you.'

'About what?'

'Can I come in?'

The gate clicked open and I walked up to the flat. The sun was coming through the windows and bouncing off the light walls.

'It's about your father.'

She nodded.

'They're searching a farm up in the mountains. It's possible something might turn up. I thought you should know.'

She smiled.

'Are you on something?' I asked.

'How do you mean?'

'You look spaced.'

'I'm fine. I just, I just want to know, you know? I've always had this terrible thought that, that he had, sort of, left me here on purpose.' She wiped away a tear with the back of her thumb. 'I'm glad it might not be true.'

'It's probably not true,' I said gently. 'Something else came up.'

'Like?'

'Your father's father. He wants to meet you.'

'How do you mean?'

'Ricky, your father, was what they used to call a love child.'

She frowned. She started shaking her head but was smiling like she didn't get it. I explained it all, about Tonin and the Salati woman. About Riccardo and his half-brothers, Umberto and Sandro. I told it all to her straight.

'So this Tonin man is my grandfather?'

'He says he is.'

'How do you mean?'

'He might be your grandfather. But if I were you I would do the tests.'

She looked at me with a face I've seen before: disappointment that the world might be so mean. I had to disappoint her further.

'There's something else you should know. This man, Massimo Tonin, is a lawyer. He might be able to look after you, but he might not. His wife and son are in custody.'

It was too much for the teenager and she broke down again. I realised I was breaking everything to a girl who needed her family around her and a branch of it was sitting in my car.

'He's outside if you want me to bring him in.'

'Who is?'

'Your grandfather.' I went out on to her balcony and pointed out my car. Tonin was sat there like a dog on a summer's day, his forlorn eyes longing for someone to let him out. I motioned with my head and he was at the buzzer in a flash.

When he came in, she didn't say anything but just looked at him.

'Elisabetta,' I said, 'this is Massimo Tonin.'

She laughed nervously.

'I'm so, so sorry I haven't . . .' he stammered.

'What?' she said.

Tonin was stumbling over lines he must have rehearsed in his head for years. 'I'm sorry all this is my fault. Your father – I didn't even know him as a son, not until the end of his life, and all I did was try to help him.

But your grandmother, she insisted I never see you. She thought I was responsible, my family was responsible, for your father's disappearance.'

She looked at me for confirmation of what he was saying.

'Silvia', Tonin said, looking at me, 'knew that my family were involved in Ricky's disappearance. She said so to me. She had nothing to prove it, and I didn't believe her until you, Castagnetti, came along this week. She said that if I ever went near her family again, Elisabetta included, she would denounce us.'

'How did she know?'

'I don't know how, but she was convinced Teresa or Sandro had done something terrible.'

Tonin looked at his granddaughter and seemed to change. 'I am your grandfather,' he said. It was the first time I had seen him smile since we had met. 'I understand if you distrust me, and you would be right to be angry at all the pain I have, inadvertently, caused you.' He was on a roll now, holding her hand. 'But I've prayed for you for years, I've thought about this moment thousands of times . . .'

I walked away. I figured they had been apart so long, they could do without someone taking notes now they were finally together.

I went outside and looked for a bar. There was a place just opposite that was busy with the football crowd. They had all assembled to watch the highlights from the day's games and were shouting insults at players they didn't like.

My phone started ringing. It was Dall'Aglio.

'We've found something.'

'Go on.'

'One of the dogs has turned up something.'

'And?'

'It's just a few bones.'

'Human?'

'We'll be doing tests.'

I took it all in. It had to be Riccardo. It couldn't be anyone else. When you go looking for a body and you find one, the identification is just a formality and Dall'Aglio knew it.

Poor boy. Murdered because he spent too much of other people's money. Hidden in the hills, forgotten by everyone except his elderly mother.

'There's something else,' Dall'Aglio said. 'We ran checks on Bocchialini and Teresa Tonin. It turns out they both spent big in the autumn of '95. He bought a car in cash, and she put down the deposit for her son's flat.'

'Cash?'

'Isn't it always?'

'Split it fifty-fifty,' I said under my breath.

'Something else,' he said. 'One of the fireflies . . .'

'The what?'

'One of the prostitutes who hang around the cittadella . . . she claims to have seen Bocchialini's car that night, parked there for an hour with him inside it.'

'She's sure?'

'She says she asked him for a cigarette, asked if he wanted company. She got a good look at his face.'

'And she's identified him?'

'That's what she says.'

'Complimenti,' I said. 'And the keys?'

'Nothing.'

'Have you searched Bocchialini's house?'

'They're still on it. They'll turn up.'

'You won't get anywhere without them. There's something else . . .'

'Go on,' Dall'Aglio said eagerly.

'Have forensics gone over the tools in Bocchialini's shed?'

'Sure.'

'Nothing of interest I take it?'

'Nothing.'

'Didn't think so. Let me tell you where you'll find the murder weapon. Or where, I'm afraid, you won't find it. A while back I was talking to the receptionist at Tonin's law firm and she was telling me how Teresa Tonin used to fill young Sandro's fridge with food. And then when we went round to the house to arrest Massimo Tonin, old Teresa was there cooking in the kitchen.'

'So?'

'It's just that she's a cook and like all good cooks she'll have all the equipment. I asked old Massimo Tonin if she has a *batticarne* and he says she uses one. But I doubt you'll find she's got one any more. She will have got rid of it after she used it on Umberto Salati on Wednesday night.'

'The tiny spikes . . .' Dall'Aglio said under his breath.

'It fits. But I fear it will only be more missing evidence . . .'

I was watching the street outside when I saw Anna di Pietro walking towards her flat with a man and a young boy. I told Dall'Aglio I had to go. I walked out of the bar and shouted over at her.

Anna looked at me with suspicion. I told her Tonin was upstairs with her daughter and she froze.

'Tonin?' She looked at me with incredulity.

'He's in there with Elisabetta now.'

'What's going on?' the man asked.

'You Giovanni?'

He nodded.

I introduced myself. The woman was already racing inside, the Standa plastic bags bouncing against her ankles as she ran.

'Anna,' I shouted.

She turned around and I walked over to her.

I told her about the farm they were searching and what they had found. She dropped her shopping.

'I'm sorry,' I said as I left them to it.

I like to think I'm a man of my word. Some wise bloke once said that it's not the oath that makes you believe the man, but the man the oath.

So when I got back to the flat I called Mazzuli from *La Gazzetta*. He came on the line spitting blood, saying I had let him down, hadn't honoured a deal we had made.

I told him I was ready to spill, just as long as my name never came up.

'Is it related to what happened to that gardener last night?'

I told it to him from start to finish. It helped clear

everything up in my mind before writing the report for Crespi. I spoke so much he didn't say a word for ten minutes. It didn't even sound like he was taking notes.

'You're sure about all this?' was all he said at the end.

'It's only hints and suppositions. It's just an informed opinion. The only difference between my job and yours is the "informed" bit.'

He laughed and muttered something about us having a drink sometime.

Telling him all about the case made me realise how incomplete it was. I went and sat in the armchair and thought it all through again. Bocchialini's suicide had, in some ways, been the ultimate act of love. With him out of the way, there was little chance Teresa Tonin would stand trial for the murder of either Ricky or Umberto. He must have known he was the only link between the dead men and the woman he loved, and he decided to eradicate the link with a bullet to the brain. We hadn't found the keys, and Dall'Aglio, I knew, was unlikely to find the weapon. Without them the only evidence connecting the woman to Ricky's disappearance was the fact that she had spent a large amount of cash back in the 1990s. Even if we did some DNA tests on Sandro, and even if we found out he really was their child, it didn't prove anything. The woman had been right when she had taunted me at her house that we had no evidence. That's the way in Italy. You have suspicions, you might even get the satisfaction of knowing who did something, and how, but the satisfaction is short-lived because you rarely see them face justice. You know, that's all, and knowledge is no good unless other people get it too.

One day something would turn up and bring me back to her. Someone would remember something, or somebody would chance across some old keys in the undergrowth somewhere. Someone would hear that rattle of metal as they walked through the woods one day and bend down to pick up the object, see the Salati surname, and remember about a murder from way back. A drought next summer might reveal a *batticarne* deep in the river bed. It might be tomorrow, it might be in ten years' time. My life was like that: a blizzard of action followed by inactivity, as I waited for fate to take its course. But I would get her one day.

The phone started ringing. I got up out of the chair half wondering if this was the missing link already. I put the phone to my ear all excited, but it was Mauro.

'You know what propolis is?' he asked.

'Sure.' It was one of the most annoying aspects of bee-keeping. It was a dark brown substance like chewing gum that the bees got from plants and used as a glue to plug holes in the hive and kill off fungal infections. My bee suit is all stained with the stuff. 'What about it?'

'I met a woman the other day who's into alternative medicine.'

'And?'

'She's looking for a source of propolis and I mentioned you. Apparently it's quite valuable.'

'It's useless to me.'

'Then sell it to her.'

'Who is she?'

'Just a woman I met.' It always amazed me how many women Mauro met.

'Bring her to the Circolo,' I said.

'I was thinking of somewhere slightly classier.'

'Bruno's then.'

We agreed to meet for dinner. The woman must have been something special because the Circolo was usually quite classy enough for Mauro. Not that Bruno's was that much better, but at least they served something other than *cotto* and *crudo*.

I was glad of the distraction. If it weren't for Mauro and my bees I wouldn't ever stop thinking about work. So Bruno's was fine by me. And besides, if we went to Bruno's there was always an outside chance I would run into Serena again. Anything's possible in a city this small.